ONE OF THE BROKEN

A DCI JAMES CRAIG NOVEL

JOHN CARSON

DCI James Craig series

DCI SEAN BRACKEN SERIES

DI FRANK MILLER SERIES

Crash Point

Silent Marker

Rain Town

Watch Me Bleed

Broken Wheels

Sudden Death

Under the Knife

Trial and Error

Warning Sign

Cut Throat

Blood from a Stone

Time of Death

Frank Miller Crime Series – Books 1-3 – Box set

Frank Miller Crime Series - Books 4-6 - Box set

MAX DOYLE SERIES

Old Habits

ONE OF THE BROKEN

 Created with Vellum

For Lisa and Gary

ONE

North Sheen Cemetery, Kew, London

Detective Chief Inspector James Craig stood in silence with the other police personnel, watching the coffin being brought out of the hearse. The fallen officer's cap was placed on top of the coffin as it was brought out by the pallbearers, men and women who had served with her.

'She was a nice lassie,' Detective Superintendent Barry Norman said to Craig.

Craig nodded, not sure he could speak without his voice cracking. Then he cleared his throat and made an effort. 'Aye, she was that, boss.'

Craig didn't look over at a small group of detectives standing over on the left, their gazes alternating between him and the coffin. One of them, a young DS who he had met before but didn't work with, had obviously been drinking before the funeral, and he kept glaring over at Craig. Ronnie Harper, if Craig's memory served him.

Harper started visibly crying when the coffin approached the freshly dug grave that was draped with fake grass, boards laid across the hole as it waited for its recipient.

'It shouldn't have been her,' Harper said. 'It shouldn't have been her!' he shouted at the top of his voice.

Norman had told Craig that Harper and the young female detective, DS Sharon Bolton, had just moved in together and were planning their future when a killer known as The Hammer had struck just weeks earlier. Her facial features had been so badly damaged by the frenzied attack that the first officers on the scene hadn't recognised her. Nobody knew that the victim had been one of their own.

Sharon had worked in Craig's Major Investigation Team, and had talked about her boyfriend – how he was a brilliant detective with another MIT, and she understood that they couldn't work on the same team.

Craig had liked her, and now knew that she had been targeted because of him – that the killer had eluded him for five years, and had played him all this time. Now he was in custody in Scotland, sitting in a room in a secure unit in a psychiatric hospital, but that was of little comfort to the grieving relatives.

None of the other officers from Craig's team stood close to him. They hadn't been happy when they found out that the killer had been known to Craig all this time, albeit without his realising it. Some of them blamed him, others just avoided him. He had seen it coming and had put in for a transfer to Police Scotland, Fife Division.

His official starting date was to be in January. Christmas was definitely not going to be the same in the Craig household this year. How could he celebrate things while this young woman would be lying in the ground? As well as the other reason.

They'd had a house to go to in Fife, left to them by his wife's uncle in Dalgety Bay. Their own house here in London had sold quickly and they had moved out shortly after. The furniture and belongings were already in Scotland. Eve had left her job and accepted a teaching job in Fife, to start when the kids went back after the break. Their new life awaited them, and attending this funeral was the last thing he wanted to do before heading back north for good. He had come down on the train and would return that way after he had said his goodbyes.

The minister had given the eulogy, his voice soothing and empathetic. The sun was out, but the cold was there, front and centre. The remnants of a snowfall leaned up against some gravestones and trees, areas that the weak sun couldn't reach. It might have looked like something out of a Victorian painting if it hadn't been for the graves, Craig thought.

Harper was even more of a wreck after he watched the pallbearers lower the coffin into the ground with the help of the gravediggers, who took the weight of the box on ropes, while the others used token symbolic ribbons.

Sharon's parents were walking back to the funeral cars when her mother stopped in front of Craig, lifted her black veil and spoke to him in a low voice.

'You bastard. You're responsible for this.' Then she spat in his face before lowering her veil, and they walked away, Sharon's father looking at Craig in disgust.

Craig took out a hanky and wiped his face.

'Yeah, why don't you fuck off back to Scotland?'

Harper shouted, and faces turned to look at him. 'Don't look at me, look at that bastard! He killed her! Just as good as! He's got blood on his hands.'

Barry Norman was over to the man in a few strides. 'My office. First thing Monday morning.' His Glaswegian accent was thick as he raised his voice.

'Oh yeah?' Harper said.

'Oh yes, sonny. You might not be in my MIT, but by Christ your boss and I will be talking about this. Now get a grip of yourself. Sharon deserves better than this.'

Norman glared at the DCI who was with Harper, and the big man led his colleague away. Then the DSup came back over to Craig.

'Don't be too hard on him, Barry,' Craig said.

'That's a damn disgrace. I know his boss. We play golf together. He couldn't be here today, but he'll be appalled when I tell him.'

'He's just in shock. I don't blame him, or Sharon's mother.' They started walking towards Norman's car.

'Grief affects everybody in different ways,' Norman said, 'but I'm damned if I'm going to let a serving officer talk to a senior officer that way, especially in public. Decorum, Jimmy, decorum.'

'Aye, but take Sharon into account too, boss.'

They got in the car and waited until the funeral cars had left, and then Norman slowly pulled away from the side of the road.

Craig looked over one last time. Sharon was alone, her friends and family leaving her behind. The gravediggers would be back later when it was quiet and they'd fill the grave in.

Craig remembered Sharon, somebody who always had a smile on her face and who would never huff and puff when she was asked to do something.

'Small mercies, I know,' Norman said, 'but at least we know The Hammer is off the streets.'

'It doesn't bring Sharon back.' Craig tore his gaze away from the grave as Norman's car moved.

'Fancy a pint?' Norman asked.

'I've got a train to catch in a few hours.'

'You've got a change of clothing in your bag in the boot of my car. You could crash at my place tonight. Deirdre won't mind. We could have a few beers somewhere we're not known. Celebrate Sharon's life.'

Craig nodded. Eve wouldn't mind if he stayed another night. She was happy to start the unpacking, and she had Finn, their German Shepherd, with her, so she wouldn't be lonely.

Christ knows, he himself felt lonely sometimes.

He had woken up several times drenched in sweat, thinking the events of just a few weeks ago were a bad dream, but then he realised they weren't. That this whole mess was as real as it got.

'Aye. Let's do it,' he said, and they left the cemetery.

And DCI James Craig left a piece of himself there with Sharon. She would never be alone and forgotten if he could help it.

TWO

Two weeks later

DCI James Craig didn't know what to expect working for the MIT in Fife, but he knew it wasn't going to be as busy as his unit in London had been.

His first day was the third of January, a bone-chillingly cold day. Unless it was just him feeling the cold, since London was a bit warmer. Fife's climate was something else he would have to get used to.

When he had popped in before Christmas, he had been told that the little office at the back was his. His predecessor, DCI Mickey Thompson, was dead, and it seemed like the man hadn't had a relationship with a can of furniture polish. In Craig's old unit, detectives were expected to clean their own environment, as no outsider was allowed into MIT.

He had made a mental note to bring his own polish and cloths, and he had today, in a bag. There was a note from DS Isla McGregor on his desk: *First day in, DCS Walker wants a word. He's always up at the crack of dawn. Don't keep him waiting.* A little smiley face was drawn there.

The police HQ was in Detroit Road in Glenrothes, a thirty-minute drive from Craig's house in Dalgety Bay. Twenty if the traffic was light and he booted his Volvo XC90 up the main road. Today, the traffic had been light and he was the first in. He was glad the old bastard – Tam – on the front desk wasn't there when he came in, but rather some young guy on the night shift, who was pleased to see some form of life. He had cornered Craig with a rundown of the events of the previous night.

Now, Craig grabbed a coffee and a bacon roll from the canteen on his way to see Bill Walker. He knocked on the office door. For an older bloke, Walker still knew how to shout, honed by years of practice shouting, 'Get the fucking door open! We know you're in there!'

'Jimmy! Come in,' Walker said, after shouting instructions for Craig to enter. 'Bloody hell, that bacon roll smells good,' he said, waving to the seat on the other side of his desk.

'You want me to go and get you one?' Craig asked.

'Christ no. Thanks anyway. My wife would kill me if she knew I was eating shite like that. She wants me trim for when I retire. It's a couple of years away, but she knows what a lazy bastard I am, and it's going to take that long for me to get to the stage where I can zip up a pair of trousers without lying on the bed first.'

'I'm watching my weight too, but a roll now and again won't kill me.'

'That's what I said to the wife. You can eat healthily for years, then go out and get hit by a bus.' Walker tutted and shook his head. 'But welcome aboard, son. It's good to have you up here, working officially.'

Craig had been up the previous month for his wife's uncle's funeral and had got caught up in a case he then helped to solve.

'I appreciate it, sir.'

'Sir, bollocks. In this office, call me Bill.'

'I had noticed that the team call DSup Baker by his first name. It's not something we do down south.'

'Ach, some people will think that's not on, but

they're a small team. They call each other by their first names in the office, but outside, they're supposed to call senior officers "sir".'

Craig was sure he'd heard them slide on that when he had been up, but he kept it to himself. 'If that's the way we work, fine by me.' It grated on him a little, but he didn't see the point of causing waves on his first day. He'd just go with the flow. Somehow, he didn't think Isla would be easy to rein in. She was full of energy, and didn't seem to let anything faze her. Maybe she was just this side of daft.

'Good man. They might use each other's first names, but they're professionals, Jimmy. I'm sure you'll find that out.'

'I have no doubt, Bill.' He ate more of his roll and washed it down with his coffee.

'How you settling in?'

'This is only my third day, but so far everything's running smoothly.'

'Good to hear.' Walker sat back in his chair and steepled his fingers. 'How's Eve doing?'

Craig made eye contact with the man. 'Honestly? She can't sleep, she feels sick and she's still in a state of disbelief at what happened, and who our son turned out to be. But she's resilient. She's starting the new teaching job and she wants to present herself as a strong figure for the kids, so she's digging deep.'

'How about you, Jimmy? How are you dealing with Joe?'

'I'm swinging between anger and shock, to be honest. I've dealt with bastards like him in London, but he's my son, and the memories of when he was a wee boy hit me right in the head.' Craig took a deep breath and let it out slowly. 'You know what he said to me, Bill?'

Walker shook his head without saying, *'Of course I bloody well don't know what he said to you.'*

'He said he never bonded with me. Because he was adopted. That shook Eve to the core. She's thinking she'll go and see a therapist, just to straighten some thoughts out.'

'Did anybody on the school board object to her taking the position after they found out what Joe was?'

'No, they've been very good. It wasn't her fault, after all.'

'Are you going to visit him in the psychiatric unit?' Walker asked.

Craig nodded. 'Eve and I are going at the weekend. We've only seen him once. Our solicitor said that the procurator fiscal wants a full rundown on his mental health before deciding if they'll prosecute him or not.'

'I don't see how they can prosecute him.'

'I don't either. He was going to kill me that night. I looked into his eyes and I didn't see my son there.'

'I read the report, Jimmy. Isla threw that big log through the living room window and Dan rushed in to help save you.'

'He's not going to let me forget it. I said I'd take him and Isla for a few beers after the New Year celebrations calmed down. I think Friday is the night we're going out. I have two days to prepare myself.'

'Dan's a good man. Isla's a good officer too, if a wee bit...quirky at times.'

'I got that impression. But she's not afraid to get her hands dirty, that's for sure.' Craig looked at Walker. 'What's your honest opinion of Max Hold?'

'Good guy. Hasn't been with us that long, but long enough to fit in. You know he came up from London like you did?'

Craig nodded. 'I do. He was in another sector. South London, I believe.'

'He came up here to do a job for a man who works for the Scottish government. Neil McGovern. You heard of him?'

'No, it doesn't ring a bell.'

13

'Alex McNeil is away to work with McGovern's department. Along with another detective's wife. I don't know much about the department, and by all accounts, I don't want to.'

'I met Alex and Harry before Christmas. I like DCI McNeil a lot.'

'Aye, I've met him too. Poor bastard went through the ringer a couple of times, let me tell you. How he gets out of bed in the morning is beyond me.'

'I think being detectives makes us think differently. We learn to compartmentalise things better. As you know from experience.'

Walker nodded. 'Aye, we do that.' His phone rang on his desk and he reached over for it, indicating with one finger that he wouldn't be a minute. 'Hello?'

Craig waited as Walker listened before answering. 'Fuck's sake, Mark, don't get your string vest in a shambles. He's in here with me. Calm yourself down, man. He'll be back down in a minute.'

Walker hung up, the receiver clattering back down. 'That was my mother.'

Craig stopped the roll halfway to his mouth.

Walker laughed. 'Jesting. That was DSup Baker.'

'I wasn't paying attention.'

'Yes you were, bloody liar. Unless you suddenly went stone deaf.'

'I might have overheard something,' Craig conceded.

'You'd be a useless detective if you hadn't. Anyway, Mark gets his boxers in a twist sometimes. He's a good bloke, don't get me wrong, but knowing him, he'd go looking for a gas leak with a box of matches.'

'Is he having a bad day?' Craig asked, finishing his roll and wiping his mouth with a paper napkin.

'Something like that. They've had a shout and he was wondering where you are.'

'What's the shout?' Craig asked, standing up.

'You know where Milton of Balgonie is?'

Craig looked stumped as he searched his mental bank of places in Fife and came up short.

'It's east of here on the A911. But if you actually arrive in Methil, you've gone too far. Get Dan to show you. He'd better bloody well know where he's going.'

'Right, I'll get going,' Craig said.

'Okay, Jimmy.' Walker looked at him. 'You feel like you've made the right move coming back to Scotland?'

Craig thought about the mother of his English

colleague Sharon spitting in his face. He nodded. 'Undoubtedly.'

'Good. Tell Eve I said hello.'

'Will do.'

Craig left the office and walked downstairs to the incident room. Baker's office was along from the room, but he was in here, pacing back and forth, running a hand through his hair, which was obviously needing a tidy-up from a young woman who would ask him if he had any holidays planned and was he doing anything special at the weekend, to which Baker would reply, no, and no. If the last hairdresser Craig had gone to was anything to go by.

'There you are, Jimmy. Thank Christ. I thought something had happened to you.'

'Like what?' Craig answered.

Baker looked at him. 'Like you had slept in or something.'

Or somebody had killed me with a hammer?

'Bill Walker asked to speak to me.'

'Yes, he told me you were up there.'

Craig saw the other team members had turned up while he was upstairs: DS Dan Stevenson and DS Isla McGregor, who he now regarded as friends; DI Max Hold, DS Gary Menzies and DC Jessie Bell.

'Right, aye, let's get along the road,' Baker said. 'Dan, you can jump in Jimmy's car. Isla, you too.'

'I'd rather just sit,' Dan replied, and Jessie sniggered.

'That's a good one, Dan,' Baker said, 'but you need new material, son.'

Dan kept chuckling as they left the incident room. He was a big man who Craig had worked with when he was a probationer in Fife twenty-five years ago.

'I think Mark's a bit stressed after the holidays,' Isla said. 'Mind you, so am I.'

'What have you got to be stressed about, Isla?' Dan asked. 'You're not married, don't have kids. You have a cat. I would love to have that kind of peace and quiet sometimes.'

'I couldn't decide what kind of ugly sweater to get Mr Boots.'

Craig looked at her and she laughed. 'I'm just kidding. I got him one with Christmas trees on it.'

'Your Volvo or my piece of crap?' Dan asked.

'Define "piece of crap",' Craig said as they entered the car park.

'Well, it's a classic, really –'

Craig put up a hand and cut Dan off mid-sentence. 'That's enough of your pish now, Dan. Classic means scrapper.'

'It's an old Land Rover Defender. I work on it myself. My old man was a mechanic and he still potters about with cars.'

'We'll take mine then. Unless Isla drives a people carrier?' Craig looked at her.

'Mini Cooper.'

He shook his head. 'It would be me or Dan going in the back, and no way am I attempting to climb into the back of one of those and risk splitting the arse of my trousers or pulling something.'

'God, don't be talking like that, boss,' Isla said, screwing up her face. 'I don't even know how we'd get you back out again.'

'The perils of being a fat bastard,' Dan chipped in.

'Listen, chubby, this is all muscle,' Craig replied.

'Listen to you two,' Isla said. 'How about instead of talking out here in the cold, we just get in your car, boss?'

'That's the first sensible thing anybody's said so far,' Craig said, blipping the remote and unlocking the car doors.

'Bagsy shotgun,' Isla said, opening the front passenger door and hopping in.

'Mother of Christ. I'll be freezing my nuts off in the back,' Dan complained.

'There's heated seats back there,' Craig told him.

'Ya beauty. Just as well, Isla,' Dan said as he got in behind her.

'Or else what?' Isla said, turning to look at him.

Dan looked at her for a second. 'Or else I'd be cold.'

'That's what I thought.'

'Crazy cat lady.'

'Right,' Craig said, starting up the car, 'I can put the address into the satnav or you can show me the way. It's Milton something-or-other.'

'Milton of Balgonie. I'll just show you.'

They headed east until they intersected with the A911. The drive took about ten minutes, and the roads were wet but light.

'It's an old church, apparently,' Dan said as Craig pulled in behind a line of emergency vehicles.

'Nice wee place,' Isla said. 'I could live somewhere quiet like this.'

Main Street ran parallel with the A911, connecting with it again at the east end. A field was opposite the house, with trees bordering it, all of it covered in snow.

Snow also covered the private car park at the side

of the old church. Boot prints formed some kind of pattern that might be called modern art somewhere. If a shitey bed could make somebody a fortune, then a snow-trampled car park shouldn't be that far behind.

'Been here before, either of you?' Craig asked as they got out of the Volvo, leaving the heat behind and stepping into a chill wind. The others were pulling in behind, each of them knowing what they had to do, DI Max Hold leading the way.

'I've passed by here, and one time I had a pint in the pub along the road, but it's not on my social calendar,' Dan said.

'Not for me,' Isla said.

Craig looked at the building; it wasn't a large church, but this village wasn't large. He wondered where they went to pray now since it had been sold.

Craig looked round. There was a VW Golf in the car park, covered in snow. He approached a uniform who was standing guard at the entrance to the car park and showed him his ID. 'Who's in there already, apart from uniforms?'

'Pathologist and the crime scene crew are in there, waiting to do their thing.'

'Get some of your team together and get the

door-to-door started,' Craig said. 'DI Hold will coordinate it.'

'Yes, sir.' The uniform moved away and Craig walked through fresh snow towards the front door.

Dan and Isla followed, and Craig could see people in white suits coming in and out of the church A woman was standing outside the front door, also wearing a white suit, but she was holding a cigarette between her lips, unlit. She clocked him walking over towards her and took the cigarette out, smiling.

'DCI Craig. The bad penny and all that.'

'Thank you, Professor. That warmed the cockles of my heart.'

The smile fell away. 'I'm sorry again about what happened. When I got to the scene, I couldn't believe it.' She was referring to the case that Craig had helped solve when he was in Fife a month earlier.

'It was a shock alright,' he said, looking at Dan and Isla, who were going into the house to give him some privacy. They put on overshoes before going out of sight.

'I made sure that the postmortem was done in Kirkcaldy. I'd only met you a short time before, but I work alongside Mark, Dan and Isla, so I wanted to be detached from that.'

'I know. I spoke to Bill Walker about it. You've been very professional about it all – everyone has. Including Stan Mackay, who I think I gave the impression of being an arsehole.'

'Not at all. Stan's a great guy. We go bowling now and again. You should come along next time. It's a work night out.'

'I will. I'll do that.' He smiled and nodded to the cigarette in her hand. 'Still having trouble, I see.'

'Oh, like you wouldn't believe. I'm a pathologist, I know how bad smoking is, but it's like trying to eat just one chocolate Hobnob.'

'I hear that.' He nodded towards the door. 'You been in yet?'

'About to go in. Come in with me and we can discover the Land of Oz together.'

They walked inside, and despite the front door being open to the elements, Craig could smell the death waiting for them. They went through the vestibule and into an area that was a living room, with other rooms off it. The gallery upstairs ran around the whole of the building.

Both Craig and Annie Keller looked over at the corpse lying on the pool table on the far side of the room. The man's face had been obliterated, and part of a pool cue was sticking out of one eye.

There was also a dead crow lying on his chest. Dead or having a lie-in, Craig wasn't sure, but he was erring on the side of it not being alive.

'Who found him?' Craig asked Dan, who had been speaking with a uniform.

'His secretary. First day back at work after the holiday. The front door was open, and when she came in, she found him like that.'

'Have you seen her yet?' Craig asked.

'I had a quick word. She's in one of the back rooms with a uniform.'

'Excuse me, gentlemen, I'd like to have a look at our victim,' Annie said, carrying her bag towards the body.

'What's his name?' Craig asked Dan.

'Vincent Donald, aged thirty-seven. Lived here alone. Not married.'

'What was his line of work?'

'Businessman. He started a software business years ago and made a fortune creating apps for phones, apparently.'

'Right. I'll talk to the secretary in a minute.'

A man wearing a protective suit came out of a room and smiled when he saw Craig. Stan Mackay, head SOCO. 'Jim. I heard you were making it official and coming back home. Glad to see you again.' He held out a fist for Craig to bump.

Craig obliged. 'Good to be back, Stan.'

'I wish we'd first met under better circumstances a month ago.'

'It is what it is, my friend,' Craig said. 'Anything disturbed?'

Mackay shook his head. 'Nothing. There's no evidence of a robbery. There's an expensive watch on the bedside table in the master bedroom upstairs, laptop, computer in the home office through there. Nothing's been touched. But there's one curious thing.'

'What's that?' Craig asked, wondering what could be more curious than the dead crow.

Mackay led Craig and Dan over to a box that contained evidence bags. He lifted one and held it up for them to see, but explained it anyway. 'A piece from a jigsaw puzzle. It was found in his hand.'

Craig couldn't quite see through the polythene bag. 'What's on it?'

'A face. A man's face.'

'Are there any jigsaws around with a missing piece that you can see?' Dan asked.

Mackay shook his head. 'I'm having one of my team look around for any jigsaw boxes, but we haven't found one yet. We don't know if the killer brought it with them or not.' He put the bag back into the box.

'Thanks, Stan.'

Craig and Dan walked over to the pool table. The green baize was covered in an oil slick that had once been red blood but had congealed in the pattern it had started but had stopped when no more had come out of the head.

'All the blood from him is on this table,' Annie said, turning to look at the detectives.

'Maybe he knew his killer and they were playing a game, and it got out of hand and he was murdered in a rage,' Dan said.

'All the balls are in the pockets,' Craig said, looking at the nets underneath each pocket. 'And that doesn't explain the jigsaw piece that was left in his hand.'

Craig stared at the man; he wasn't overweight, he had a good head of hair and he was dressed in smart clothes. There was a Rolex on his left wrist. And Mackay had said he had another expensive watch upstairs.

'How did the secretary know this was her boss?' Craig said to Dan. 'I mean, there's nothing left of his face.'

'She assumed. She said she saw him lying on the table and called us. She ran out to her car and got in it, starting it up and getting ready to take off if a stranger came out of the house. And, in her words, "I was ready to run the bastard over."'

'I don't blame her,' Annie said. 'I thought the same thing about my ex-husband. But he wouldn't have put that to the test.'

'He probably figured you knew multiple places where you could stab him to have the most effect,' Craig said, and while the hairs on the back of his neck weren't exactly standing up, they were certainly waiting on the starter's pistol.

'Exactly,' Annie said. She looked at the body. 'I was going to say we might need dental records to identify him, but there's a chance that his teeth have been affected and knocked out of place. That cue will be a bugger to cover up when we get him out of here. We'll need the mortuary van to be backed up as close to the door as possible. I'll give them a call in a minute.'

'We'll run his prints for a proper identification,' Craig said. 'If you can do that, Dan.'

'Boss.'

Craig looked at Annie. 'Time of death?'

She looked at him. 'I'd say roughly six hours ago,

seven tops. Not much more than that.' She looked at her watch. 'Around three or four this morning.'

'Thanks, Annie. Now I'd like to talk to the secretary. What room is she in?' he asked Dan.

Dan pointed over to where a door stood open. 'It's an office.' There was a uniform standing outside of it. Craig went over and gave his name before entering the room. A female uniform was with the young woman. Craig was expecting tears and an abundance of paper hankies, but what he saw was a young woman staring into space.

'I'm DCI James Craig,' he said to her. 'And you are?'

'Cindy,' she replied.

Craig indicated for the uniform to leave the room, and the young officer got up and left the two of them to it.

'Last name?' Craig said. 'How about the one you were given at birth?'

He studied the woman as they locked eyes; she looked to be about mid-twenties and was thin without seeming like she regularly missed meals. Her hair was blonde, from a bottle. Her cheekbones were pronounced, and her lips were full, but not with Botox.

'Cindy Moore.' She was sitting in an armchair,

facing him. He quickly scanned the office, but there was nothing in here that a million other home offices didn't have: a desk with a closed laptop on it; a leather office chair; prints on the walls; a printer sitting on top of a two-drawer filing cabinet.

Craig stood looking at her, keeping his hands in his pockets. 'So, Cindy Moore, why don't you tell me what happened?'

She looked away again. 'Look, I didn't kill the cocky bastard; I just found him like that.'

'You didn't like him, then?' Craig said, barely disguising the sarcasm in his voice.

'I bet there are people you've worked for you didn't like. It doesn't mean you killed them,' she countered.

Craig admitted to himself that she had a point. There were several bigwigs in London that he would have crossed the road to avoid, but he wouldn't have thrown a toaster in their bath. How he would have been in a position to be holding a toaster while one of the bosses was naked in a bathtub he couldn't quite put his finger on.

'Cocky bastard? Can you elaborate?' Craig said.

'I'm sure you've met some of them in your time too.'

I'm talking to one now, he thought, but kept that to himself. 'You tell me first,' he said instead.

'Look, I want nothing to do with this. I just want to go home.'

'I'd rather you stay and answer some questions.'

'Am I a suspect?'

'Number one, until we determine one way or the other,' Craig said.

'Christ. Look, he was just somebody I met and he asked me if I wanted to do some secretarial job, part time. I said okay, and I came in now and again to help him with paperwork.'

'When did you meet him?'

'A couple of months ago.'

'And you weren't planning on staying long?' Craig said.

'This was a stopgap. I didn't enjoy it, but he paid well. I just didn't like him. But as for doing that to him? Oh God, no.'

He looked at her. He had come across clever killers before, like the ones who murdered somebody, went away and got changed, and came back hours later to 'discover' them. Cindy didn't strike him as one of them.

'Where did you meet him?'

'In a pub in Glenrothes. He seemed nice then,

but I soon saw he's always stressed out, shouting at people on the phone. I can't imagine anybody working for him for a long time.'

He asked her a few more questions but didn't get the feeling she was responsible. They'd run her through the system anyway.

Craig left the office and walked over to Dan. He looked back at the office door, then at the DS. 'Get her down to the station. We'll interview her later. Get Isla to see what she can find out about this Cindy Moore. If that's her real name.'

Dan nodded and went in search of Isla. Across the room, Annie Keller was poking and prodding. Craig walked over to her. 'I was going to make a joke about an old crow but thought better of it. I remembered you know how to use a scalpel,' he said to her.

'I wouldn't use a scalpel on you, Jimmy. Women prefer poison.' She was looking at the broken pool cue still sticking out of the man's eye socket. The bird was equally untouched.

'If I ever get round to being in your mortuary, remind me not to accept a coffee.'

'Oh, you'll find yourself there. They all do. And then you're mine, Craig.' She shook her head. 'Old crow indeed.'

Craig grinned.

Annie stood up. 'I could take this out here, but I would rather do it when he's on my table.'

'We should get some uniforms to hold up tarps as he's being taken out. I didn't see any press outside, but nowadays, everybody has a camera in their pocket.'

'That would be great, Jimmy. Give the man a wee bit of dignity as he's taken out. Not that he'll care, but still.'

Craig stared at the crow on the man's chest. He knew crows were a sign of death, and that one lying there, dead, didn't bode well at all.

THREE

Eve thought, *If anybody else says how fucking sorry they are, I'll spit nails.*

She was glad they were sympathetic, but deep down, she knew they were glad it hadn't happened to them.

She'd called Joe, her son, the previous night, but she wasn't sure who she would be talking to. Him or his alter ego. He had dissociative identity disorder. The psychiatric unit were very good, of course, but she couldn't force her son to talk if he didn't want to.

She was sitting in the staffroom having a coffee when her friend Rose Dempsey came in.

'Getting everything organised?' Rose said, grabbing herself a coffee.

'Like riding a bike,' Eve said. 'London's not too

different. I just need to make slight adjustments for up here.'

'It'll be like a Taylor Swift concert when they come back tomorrow.'

Eve smiled. 'I'm looking forward to it. It'll be a huge distraction for me.'

'Sometimes the girls and I go out for a drink on a Friday. Not clubbing, mind you, just a few social drinks. You can come along if you like.'

'I'll take a rain check, if you don't mind. Lots on my mind just now.'

'Oh God, aye. Any time you change your mind, just let us know. They're a pretty good bunch here.'

'I've still to meet some of the others, but they seem friendly.'

Rose came over and sat down at the table next to Eve. 'When are you going to see Joe again?'

'Jim and I are going over on Saturday to see him.'

'If you need a shoulder to cry on, let me know. You were here for me when I got divorced, and I'll always be here for you.' Rose reached out a hand and put it on Eve's.

'Thank you.'

They sat and chatted about the work they had to do at home to prepare for the kids coming.

FOUR

Craig had always been intrigued by churches that had been put out to pasture and sold off, then were refurbished and sold as houses. No wonder the Church was losing worshippers. Where were they supposed to go to worship when somebody had decided the buildings must go? Maybe they thought that online worshipping would be cheaper.

This church had been small, but big enough for the village. He climbed the spiral staircase to the gallery level and slowly walked around. This was where the bedrooms were. Nothing remarkable about them, except they were a good size, not like the new houses where broom closets were now called bedrooms.

The master bedroom had a huge bed in it. And

the other expensive watch Stan Mackay had mentioned. A Breitling.

There were photos in frames on a dresser, showing a man – Donald, Craig assumed – on a beach somewhere, with a young blonde woman posing with an arm around his shoulders, a palm tree and blue sea in the background. There were three photos taken in what appeared to be the same location at different times of the day, with the couple wearing beachwear and then attire for going out for an evening.

Craig took out his phone and took photos of the photos. Was the woman the next of kin? She was obviously special to Donald. He walked back out onto the gallery, where there had once been seats and the parishioners could look down on the minister below.

More photos on the wall, but landscapes this time. A photo of a lighthouse, but not in Scotland. Somewhere in America, judging by the car over to one side. Donald seemed to have been an intelligent man, but owning a tech business might have made him enemies.

Craig walked forward and looked over the gallery to the body lying on the table below. Annie looked up at him and smiled. He smiled back. He'd met some arsehole pathologists in his time, and coroners too, and it made a pleasant change to meet somebody like Annie.

His phone dinged and he stepped away from the wooden wall and took his phone out, thinking it was his wife, but he saw it wasn't.

It was Carrie Dickson, his son's girlfriend. Or ex-girlfriend now, he supposed.

'Carrie,' he said, answering the phone.

'Sorry to call you, Jim. I just needed to talk to you. Is there any chance we could meet up for a coffee?'

Craig looked at his watch. 'Yes, I can meet you, but I can't be long. We're in the middle of an investigation.'

'I won't keep you long.'

'Where are you just now?' Craig asked.

'I'm at home. I'm selling up and moving.'

'I'm in Glenrothes just now.'

'Oh. That's fine then. It doesn't matter.' She sounded disappointed, but Craig knew it was more than that: the young woman was gutted. Perhaps she had seen a future with Craig's son; maybe she'd seen Craig as her future father-in-law. Now it was all in the past as that future with Joe was never going to happen.

'Look, I'll make the time. I'll just hand over here and come down. Say, half an hour?'

'That's fine, Jim. I appreciate it. I'll get the kettle on. You remember where I live?'

How could I forget? Craig had been to her house with his wife and son, after Carrie's grandfather had died there. 'Yes, of course. See you soon.'

He hung up and made his way down the spiral staircase, which was designed to confuse the unwary and try to break their neck. If he'd had vertigo, it would have been a better day out than getting blootered at the pub.

Back on solid ground without making a spectacle of himself, Craig walked over to Annie. 'I have to go and see somebody.'

The pathologist held up a hand. 'You're not going to leave me here with all these other people, are you? Please don't leave me, Jim. I was only kidding about the coffee.'

'Alas, I have to go. Maybe I'll return. Maybe I'll find pastures new. Who knows?'

'Go then. Make it quick and painless.' She grinned, and for a brief moment, Craig wondered if she was a secret drinker.

Why did you flirt with her? he asked himself, and not finding an answer, he doffed an imaginary hat and turned to leave. Then he saw Isla standing talking to a uniform. He walked over to them.

'I have to go out. There are photos in frames in a bedroom upstairs, of a man and a woman. If that's definitely the owner of this place, find out who the woman is. Take a photo of them and ask his secretary if she knows. Then let me know. I'll see you back at the station.'

'Yes, sir.'

'Have patrol take you and Dan back.'

'Okay, no problem.'

As Craig left, he turned round to look at Annie. She was busy looking at the crow.

FIVE

Craig found a parking space along from Carrie Dickson's house in Kirkcaldy. Snow was lying up against walls in front of houses, and the cold wind made his eyes water.

There was a For Sale sign in front of the house with the name of an estate agent on it.

Carrie answered the door after the first knock. She smiled at Craig, but it was the sad version people kept in reserve for such occasions as asking the spouse of a dead person if they were doing okay.

'Come on in, Jim.'

He nodded and stepped into the heat of her hallway, picturing the time he had been here with Eve and Joe, a few weeks previously, but it seemed like years ago now.

Carrie closed the front door behind her and Craig stood looking at her.

'Let's go through to the kitchen,' she said to him and he followed her. He looked at the bottom of her stairs, where her grandfather had been found dead, then carried on.

'The kettle's just gone off,' Carrie said, pouring the hot water into two mugs that already had instant coffee in them. 'Milk and sugar?' she asked as Craig sat down at the dining table.

Taking milk in coffee in somebody else's house was always hit or miss. How fresh was it? Did it look like it had cottage cheese in it?

'Black's fine, thanks,' he replied and watched her stir it.

She sat at the table with the two mugs and Craig took his, enjoying the hot liquid. He waited for Carrie to explain why she wanted to see him, but she just looked into her mug.

Craig wanted to say something without it sounding facetious. He finally came out with, 'You wanted a chat?'

She looked at him and nodded. 'I got a call from Joe.'

Thoughts ran through his head; he wondered why his son had called her. She had been his girlfriend just a few weeks ago, but since he had been put in the psychiatric hospital, that had been the end of the road for that relationship.

'What did he want?' Craig asked, knowing his son swung back and forth between his multiple personalities.

She sniffed as she started to cry a little bit. 'He said he didn't know why he was in the hospital, and when was I going to go and get him. I didn't want to come right out and tell him he wasn't going to get out.'

'They're still evaluating him. There are a lot of reports to be written, reports to be made, but you were right not to say anything to him. You don't know how he's going to take it. Or if the other personality will take over.'

Carrie fought the tears and drank some coffee. 'He wants me to go and visit him.'

'That's not going to be possible. Nobody's allowed to go and see him except his mother and me. We're going in on Saturday. But nobody else is allowed, except his solicitor, and only then when he's escorted by hospital staff, who are basically bodyguards.'

'It's a real mess, Jim, isn't it? I miss him. We were getting on so well.'

Craig drank some coffee. 'Was there ever any sign of what was lurking inside?'

She shook her head. 'No. Was there any for you?'

It was a question, but also a retort. How could he be Joe's father and not know what had been going on inside him?

'No. He masked it very well.'

'Well, we both know he had help.'

'At least one of them is in prison,' Craig replied, anger in his voice. Then he changed the subject. 'Have you had any offers on your house yet?'

'Yes. It was quiet over the holiday period of course, but now that's over, people are looking in earnest.'

'This is a nice area. You shouldn't have any problem.'

Carrie looked around the kitchen as if remembering a different time when people had been happy and laughter had filled the room instead of tears.

'We were going to live here, Joe and I,' she said. 'Eventually. But now it's all down the toilet.'

'Are you looking to buy a new place?' Craig asked.

'I'm not sure yet, to be honest. I'm going to rent for a little while before deciding if I want to own something else. You know, keep my options open.'

'We were lucky that Clark left us his house in Dalgety Bay. We would have bought something either way because our house in London didn't stay on the market for long.' He drank more coffee. 'Are you staying in the area?'

'I'm not sure, to be honest. I thought about maybe moving over to Edinburgh. I'm not giving up on Joe.'

'It could be a long time before you ever see him again. If at all.'

'Maybe I should have seen the signs. I feel guilty.'

'You've nothing to feel guilty about, Carrie.'

'Thanks, Jim. But if I can be near him, then I won't feel I've just abandoned him.'

'Can I ask you: did he ever have an epileptic fit when he was with you?'

She looked at him and nodded. 'Yes. A few times over the relatively short period of time I was with him.'

Craig nodded. 'It started when he was a little boy. Since Joe was taken away to the hospital, we've been doing some research, and some places think that his epilepsy could have triggered the disassociate disorder. I think the solicitor will argue that with the PF's office.'

'Will they let him go?' Carrie asked hopefully.

Craig shook his head. 'He murdered people. They're not just going to let him walk the streets. He's got a long way to go.'

'I won't give up on him, Jim. I have never felt this way about a man before, and just because he's been taken away from me, I won't let him down.'

'I'm sure he would appreciate that.'

'Will you tell him when you see him at the week-end? That I won't let him down? That he's the only one for me?'

Craig nodded. 'I will.' He looked at his watch. 'I'd better get up to the station.' He stood up, and smiled at her, thinking that Joe was a lucky man to have a woman this dedicated by his side.

Carrie stood up and came round to hug him. 'I'm not going to leave your life, Jim. I want to keep in touch.'

'That's good,' he said.

She smiled at him as he walked out of the house.

SIX

Craig stood looking at the board in the incident room. At the jigsaw puzzle piece, which was part of a blown-up photo.

'It looks like an old photo,' Isla said. 'Like somebody found a box of them in the attic and decided to have it blown up and made into a jigsaw puzzle.'

'Could be.' He looked at Max Hold. 'Have you found a next of kin yet?'

Max, Jessie and Gary Menzies had suspended the job they were working on to lend a hand in the incident room. Dan was sitting at another computer.

'Not yet. Gary's our whizz on the computer. He can't find anything on Vincent Donald's private life in our system.'

'Except one thing,' Gary said.

'Except one thing,' Max repeated. He looked at Gary. 'Don't keep us in suspense then, Gary.'

'A reunion that's being organised on Facebook. Some friends from St Andrews University getting together.'

'Where's it being held?' Craig asked.

'At a hotel in South Queensferry. The Dakota. In the bar.'

'Who's organising it?'

Gary looked at his screen. 'Penelope Sandilands. That was her name back then. She's Penelope Armstrong now.'

Craig looked at Isla. 'Did you find out anything about the woman in the photos?'

'I asked some neighbours about her, and they said her name was Susan Renwick.'

'Was?' Craig said.

'Yes. She's dead. They lived together for a couple of years. A whirlwind romance, by all accounts. They were planning on getting married apparently, but then Susan died.'

'How long ago?'

'A few weeks ago,' Gary said. 'Tenth of December.'

'Christ, that was some Christmas for Donald,' Craig said.

'Did they say how she died?' Dan asked.

'She died in a car crash, driving along a country road,' Isla said. 'When the accident reconstruction team looked at it, they found plastic in the middle of the road from broken lights. It looked like her car had been hit at the back right corner, ramming it off the road.'

'Deliberate or an accident?' Max asked.

Isla looked at him. 'It could have been either, but the traffic unit had seen crashes like this before, mostly from boy racers losing control, but also from a drunk driver hitting another car. Maybe it was somebody overtaking at high speed, not realising there was a bend in the road going right. Either way, it looked like she'd been hit and the car rolled several times, and she was killed.'

Craig nodded. 'Nobody else was at the scene when the police arrived?'

'Correct,' Isla said. 'There were no witnesses, nobody else travelling on the road. It was early evening, but very quiet. Besides, it was raining, it was dark, and they figured that speed was a factor.'

'Did anybody question Vincent Donald?' Dan asked.

'Yes. Officers from the traffic unit questioned him later. They clocked his Golf and saw no damage to it, and he was in the restaurant waiting for her when it happened. She'd gone to see her father, who was ill, and told Donald she would meet him there.'

'What day of the week was the tenth?' Craig asked.

'A Sunday. It says on the report.'

'What restaurant?' Craig asked.

'The Foxton, not far from here. It was quiet that night and the waitress said she remembered him being there because she felt sorry for him, being stood up. He waited forty-five minutes, telling her he couldn't get hold of his girlfriend. Then, as he left, he asked the waitress to tell her he'd gone home if she turned up,' Isla said.

'Didn't he have her parents' number?' Max asked.

'Her mother is dead, so it was just her father. It doesn't say, but if he did, why didn't he call it after waiting forty-five minutes? Even if it was just to check up on Susan.'

'Let's assume he didn't, then,' Craig said. 'When was he informed about the crash?'

'They weren't sure how long the car had been in the trees, but they guessed an hour or more. Nobody came forward to say they'd seen anything, but fair play, the car lights didn't stay on. He got the death message about two hours after the accident.'

'Reaction?'

'Completely broke down. The uniform said that Donald was devastated.'

'Find out if there was any life insurance payout and if Donald was the recipient if there was.'

'Are you thinking foul play, sir?' Jessie asked.

'You never know. If there was and Donald wasn't involved, then maybe whoever killed him also killed his girlfriend. Or maybe a member of her family thought Donald killed her and took revenge on him. I don't want to speculate, but we need to cover all angles.'

Craig turned to Isla. 'Find out who Susan's next of kin was, if she had one. We can go and talk to whoever it was, if there was somebody. If they're still alive. You mentioned her father, but just check to see if he's alive. Either way, check the report. A name would be in there.'

'Will do.'

Max stood up straighter and stretched his back. 'We asked neighbours if they saw people coming round to Donald's house. He did have friends though. There was a little group of them. Four. They were drinking in the local bar over Christmas, so we know it was recent.'

'Any names?'

'One of them was Badger, the bar owner said when we went to talk to him. He thinks the other one was Mason. The third friend was Crystal. He said Donald was the worse for wear, but they were celebrating Susan's life. Then Donald broke down and they took him home.'

'Get a search warrant for Donald's house, just to keep everything above board,' Craig said. 'See if there's anything in there like an address book or something.'

'I'll get that organised,' Max said.

'Good man.'

'I think you and I should go for a night out on Saturday, sir,' Isla said to Craig, smiling.

'Really now? I don't know what my wife would have to say about that,' Craig answered, feeling like his tadger was being pulled.

She laughed. 'I meant we should gatecrash this shindig the social media crowd have got organised at The Dakota. I'm sure they'll be upset at the news of Donald's passing, but they won't let that stop the show from going on. Young people are so superficial nowadays.'

'Says Granny Isla,' Dan chimed in.

'Och, away with yourself, Heid-the-Baw. You know what I meant.'

'I'm sure you just violated some workplace rule there. I'm going to have to find a safe place now. Keep my heid down for a wee while until you all make me feel better again.'

'Buy a box of doughnuts, Dan; that'll make you feel good again,' Jessie said, grinning.

'Everybody's a comedian,' Dan said, shaking his head.

'There's more about this Facebook meeting,' Gary said. He was working on his computer. 'It seems that Donald was going to be giving some sort of speech. He was a tech whizz, and had started his own company, developing apps and software. He was due to be given an award from some finance group. Apparently, Donald helped underprivileged kids.'

'As hard as I'm trying, I can't find a motive in there,' Craig said. 'His girlfriend dies, and he shares his money helping kids. He seems like he was a decent bloke.' Craig looked at the others. 'I wonder why he chose to live in a little one-horse town?'

'It's really a village,' Gary said.

'And they called us. They want their idiot back,' Isla said.

Gary looked up from his computer. 'What are you waiting for then?'

'That was actually quite good, Menzies,' she replied. 'You should be proud of yourself.'

Craig looked at Isla. 'Where was the crash site, where Susan Renwick died?'

'On the A916, at the junction where the road goes to Leven. The B927.'

'Right then, let's see if we can find some people to talk to.'

SEVEN

Craig sat in his office looking at the computer, which looked old enough to have witnessed the first moon landing. He was reading the report on Susan Renwick's crash. It was a Sunday night and she'd been on her way to the restaurant from her dad's' house in Cupar and had gone off the road into the woods at high speed. She was dead by the time the fire brigade cut her out.

Craig opened up Google Street View and looked at the site where Susan had died. He moved the view up and down the road and looked at the view from the direction she had been travelling coming back from her dad's' house. It was a long, straight section of road, bordered by a wall on one side and trees on the other. There was a warning sign outside a house indicating the junction ahead, but he could imagine somebody getting up to a fast speed on that stretch, especially if they were familiar with it and were over-confident. Then add the darkness and the rain into the mix and it could be a recipe for disaster, as it clearly had been for Susan.

Isla came over and stood by his desk. 'I found the next of kin for Susan Renwick in the accident report, sir.'

Craig looked at her; first Bill Walker said that they called each other by their first names here, then Isla started calling him 'sir'. Was that because she was in front of the others, or was she playing mind games with him? He didn't care. Back in London when he worked with the Met, they would call each other by their first names when they were out on the lash, so maybe that was what was happening here.

'You said earlier her dad lives in Cupar,' he said, taking the sheet of paper from her.

'I did indeed. Uniform did the death message. Both of them, the father and the boyfriend. The case is still open as they try and figure out if she was hit by a drunk driver.'

'Did Gary find out anything about an insurance policy?'

'Hold on, I'll ask him.'

Craig expected her to walk away from his desk, but she went to the office door and shouted over, 'Gaz! Insurance policy on Susan Renwick?'

'Jesus, Isla, could you shout it a wee bit louder? I don't think Edinburgh heard you.'

Isla turned to Craig and laughed. 'Sorry, boss. Gary has selective hearing.' She turned to look back into the incident room, and watched Gary get off his chair and walk over to her.

'I just printed this out. The insurance company wanted a final report from us before paying out. The pathology report indicated accidental death. Blunt force trauma to the head. She wasn't wearing her seatbelt. There's a one-hundred-thousand-pound policy. Beneficiary was her father, not her boyfriend. The insurance company haven't paid out yet until they get a final report from the accident investigation unit, but it's a formality.'

'Good work, both of you.' Craig stood up from behind his desk. 'Isla, grab your jacket.'

Gary walked back to his desk. Isla looked at Craig. 'Early lunch, or...?'

'Or. We're going to talk to Susan's father. First, though, call ahead and see if they're in.'

'Two minutes.'

55

She came back when Craig was putting his jacket on. 'I called and the father's in. Lou Renwick is his name.'

'Let's go.'

EIGHT

Cain stood over the sink, letting the water from the tap run over the dried blood on the blade, staring out of the kitchen window at the snow-covered trees outside.

He sensed the movement behind him as his brother scuffed his foot on the flagstone floor. Cain wondered if his sibling did this deliberately because he knew what would happen if he got too close and surprised him. Then again, Abel thought he was the hardest out of them both. Maybe one day they'd put it to the test and find out for sure.

Not today, though. Cain was tired after last night's fun.

'Morning, mucker,' Abel said, coming into the

kitchen wearing nothing but his skids and vest, and scratching his arse.

'Fuck's sake, somebody could see you parading about like that,' Cain said, turning to his brother.

Abel laughed. 'Don't talk pish. Who's going to see me out here? A haggis running wild out in the garden?' He chuckled again and switched the kettle on. Without washing his hands first, dirty bastard, Cain thought.

He carried on washing the blood off the knife. It was an army combat knife, black with a serrated top edge and a razor-sharp cutting edge. Cain sharpened it every day, coddling it like a mother might coddle her baby. It was a thing of beauty to behold and admire, like a fancy painting down in the galleries.

'You ate yet?' Abel said.

'Not yet, and seeing you in here in your manky fucking skids is ruining my appetite.'

Abel laughed again. 'Christ, my Ys are putting you off your breakfast, but ripping that guy apart with your knife keeps your beans down. I'll never understand you.'

'Nobody will ever understand me.'

Cain wiped the blade with his fingers, careful not to slice one open. The victim's blood ran down with the water, making a hasty escape down the plug hole. If a fancy expert like the ones on the telly came in here and took apart his sink, and skooshed their liquid around here and turned out the lights and used the black-light torch, they would have a field day. But he wouldn't let them come in here and take their place away. He'd burn the place down before he let that happen. If they weren't sneaky and just turned up with a search warrant. But the first one through the door with the piece of paper in his hand would die first, because by then it would all be over.

He ran through the events of last night in his head again, feeling the adrenaline rush starting to kick in.

It was snowing hard, which meant driving was treacherous, but where was the fun if you weren't shitting yourself?

It was like going up on a roller coaster even though you hated the things, listening to those lying bastards when they said it didn't look like you were up too high when you were right at the top. The chain rattled and things clanked underneath and the wind caught your hair. Then the car sat there at the apex and you convinced yourself it was going to be alright. It started to creep forward and then started to go over, and you knew there was absolutely nothing on earth you could do to stop it now, and it was going and taking you with it. Then the feeling like you were freefalling, but you weren't – you were in a little roller coaster car on a track that somebody had built, maybe somebody who had been drinking at lunchtime, and now was the time a bolt was going to come loose and you were firing down this track feeling like you were about to die at high speed.

They lied to you just so you would do what they wanted. And here you were, the adrenaline coursing through your body, not giving you time to think –

'You okay?' Abel asked him.

Cain looked at his brother. 'Of course I'm okay. Just concentrate on the road.' He watched the small windscreen wipers bat at the snowflakes.

'You looked like you were back there again. In a land far away.' Abel grinned.

'Shut up. I was going through the plan in my head. Like you should have been doing. Trying to think about what could go wrong and how we would deal with it.'

'I was just saying.' The smile was gone now as Abel gripped the steering wheel.

Cain glared at his brother for a second, feeling

the rising anger, but then he fought it down, keeping it at bay. He felt that he could talk to Abel that way since he, Cain, was the oldest. By four minutes.

It had been a close one, their mother had said. They had almost been born in different years as midnight had approached, but then Abel had decided to make his entrance and saved the day.

Abel had saved the day, as always. Abel was the good son, even though he looked exactly like his brother. Same smile, same hair, same height (although the bastard always cheated when they had put the ruler on top of each other's heads to mark the spot on the doorframe and see how tall they were). Cain knew Abel was his mother's favourite. What had he done to deserve that accolade? Nothing that Cain could think of.

The Land Rover slid sideways a bit and Cain jerked his head round to look at his brother, just to make sure he was still awake.

Abel grinned in the darkness of the car, showing off the same good set of teeth that Cain had.

'What's wrong?' Abel said. 'Got to change your underwear now?'

'You're hilarious. Just keep your eyes on the fucking road.' Although the road looked more like a ski slope than anything else.

Abel chuckled. Cain shook his head. Everything between them was a competition, and each of them thought they were the better driver. The only reason Abel was driving was because he'd won the coin toss.

'I always said you were a tosser,' he had said, laughing, as the coin landed on heads.

Same for this job tonight. Heads or tails. This time it was tails. Cain was a control freak, and he had clenched his fists to stop himself from poking his own eyes out at the thought of giving his brother control, letting him drive. But he had let him take the keys, wishing he had cheated on the coin toss.

Cain just wanted to make sure tonight went smoothly. They couldn't afford to have things go sideways. He would let his brother drive, but there was no way Cain was going to let him control tonight's event, not after Abel almost lost control of the Land Rover when they had run that bitch off the road. Cain had let out a 'fuck me' when the big car had hit the smaller one, just at the point where Abel had fought with the steering wheel and brought the car back on course. He had laughed then, thinking it was funny, and Cain had sat quietly, not wanting to open the floodgates and start an argument. Or worse, stab his brother in the eye with a combat knife.

'Go right down the M90 so we can connect with the A92.'

'What's wrong with the A911 at Milnathort?' Abel asked.

'Are ye daft? Are you looking out the same windscreen I'm looking out of, or are there cartoons playing in front of your eyes in your world? Look at the fucking weather.'

'What's going on in *your* heid?'

Cain pointed out of the windscreen. 'That's what's going on in my fucking heid. If we took the A911, we could go off the road, and then what? The polis ask us where we were going, that's what.'

'We could end up going off this road.'

'I'm not asking you to drive on the surface of the moon. Just stick to the main roads and we'll have a better chance of getting to our destination without the fire brigade cutting us out of the car.'

'We could slide off these roads too, half-wit.'

'What did you say?'

'Nothing,' Abel mumbled. The wipers battled the snow. If it were summer, they'd have got there in half the time, but the roads were treacherous and the weather was perfect for keeping people indoors. It was only madmen and hardened killers like them who were out and about.

Getting to the village was more of a challenge as they left the main road, Abel commenting that he should have put his brown trousers on.

'Told you,' Cain said. 'If we'd gone the tourist route, you would have been bricking it.'

'Only if you were driving.'

'Pay attention, the turn's coming up on your right.'

'Why don't we get a satnav thing we can stick on the window?'

Cain tutted. 'We've spoken about this before. Those things leave trails inside, so the police can look at where you've been.'

'We could always take it with us when we leave,' Abel said, making the turn and correcting the heavy vehicle as it slid sideways.

'Too risky. They might find it if they come looking. Just keep your eyes on the road.'

'I'm hardly looking out the back window.'

'Shut up, sarky bastard. The last thing we need is for you to put this thing through a hedge.'

He turned left into the street they were looking for. A pub was on their left, now in darkness since the last of the patrons had left hours ago.

'It's up on the left,' Cain said, pointing, in case

Abel had suddenly found himself devoid of all sense of direction.

Abel slowed, looking in the mirrors. Seeing nothing behind, he pulled into the church car park. Cain had told him that even if they did manage to find tyre treads, they wouldn't be unique to their car.

Abel slowed down and parked next to the snow-covered Golf and turned the engine off immediately.

They were both wearing woollen caps and they pulled them down a bit further on their heads, before Cain took the two warrant cards out of his pocket. He opened them and handed Abel his.

'How come I'm the DS and you're the DI?'

'I'm older, remember, bawbag. Now, stop your whining and let's get this job done.' Cain looked at his card: Detective Inspector Ross Naylor. His brother was DS Jack Naylor.

They got out of the car, not closing the doors all the way, and walked through the snow to the side of the house where the entrance was. Cain was in the lead, Abel following closely behind. They had the collars up on their jackets and kept their heads down.

Cain knew a lot of people had camera doorbells, but he had already scoped the house out and the owner didn't have one. Cain supposed the occupant thought he was safe in a little village, figuring house-breakers weren't rampant there.

He knocked hard on the door, not hard enough to alert neighbours – although the neighbour to the left was a school – but hard enough hopefully to wake the man inside.

Just when he thought he would have to hammer on the wood even harder, the light above their heads came on. A few seconds later, they heard a wary voice from behind the door.

'Who is it?'

'Police, Mr Donald. We need to speak to you.' Cain thought it was always a good touch to use their name, get them thinking he wasn't just some random stranger who had walked in off the road and was about to tan their house.

The door opened a crack with a chain on, which was superb. That way, both men could shove their warrant cards into the gap for Donald to read them. They were real, supplied by a man in London for a very hefty price. The names were real too, serving officers in the Met, so they were covered if somebody called and asked, *Do you have detectives called Naylor there?* The Met wouldn't just give out the names, but it would make the caller feel a little more comfortable.

It had worked every time, except once, when they had visited a fat bastard called Marco who didn't believe them and had put up a hell of a fight before Cain shot him in the head.

It seemed that Vincent Donald had no such qualms about opening his door, and he stood aside to let them into the small vestibule. Cain wondered if this had been where the minister had greeted his flock. He had never set foot inside a church, so he wouldn't know the ins and outs, but it certainly smelled like he imagined a church would. Maybe the years of candle burning had seeped into the wood.

Either way, Donald accepted them for what he thought they were, and closed the door behind them.

'Please go through into the warmth,' he said. He was wearing a dressing gown over pyjamas.

'Working late?' Abel asked.

'I'm a night hawk,' Donald said. 'I don't sleep very well.'

Inside the open space that was now the living room, Donald stood looking at them. 'What's this all about?'

'We work down in London, and we've arrested a man we believe murdered Susan,' Cain said, the statement designed to knock the man off balance.

'What? Murdered? Oh my God. I thought that was an accident. Christ, this is awful.'

'Can we sit down for a moment?' Cain asked.

'Yes, of course.' Donald looked stunned, which pleased Cain.

They walked over to an L-shaped couch and sat down near each other.

'Do you think I could use your toilet, sir?' Abel said.

'Yes, of course. It's the blue door over there.' Donald pointed vaguely in the direction of the bathroom.

Abel got up, and that was when it hit Donald. 'You look exactly alike.'

Which was why they used warrant cards that had the same last name on them, so if anybody questioned this, they could say they were brothers. That was usually the end of it.

'Hence the same last name,' Cain said.

'I didn't really take notice.'

'Nobody does.' Cain watched his brother go into the bathroom.

'Somebody killed my Susan?' Donald said, as if that was the first time he'd been told.

'I'm afraid so. He's a serial killer.'

'Good God.' Donald looked at Cain. 'Have you told her dad?'

'Not yet. We were hoping you could give us an address. Is her mother still around?'

Donald shook his head. 'She died years ago. Her father is still around. I can get you his address.' He made to get up, but Cain put out a hand.

'We can get that before we leave. But I'd like to ask you to get dressed so you can come along to Glenrothes station with us. They've got photo ID books there, waiting. We believe the man who murdered your girlfriend is known to you.'

Donald's mouth dropped open for a second. 'Jesus. Do you have a name?'

'We do. But we can't influence you. We want you to take a look at the books and see if you can pick him out.'

Donald stood up. 'I'll go and get dressed now.' He walked over and climbed the spiral staircase, and Cain waited until he heard a door close upstairs before standing up.

Abel came out of the bathroom. 'I'll go and get the bag.'

Cain looked at his watch. 'Hurry up. We don't have long,' he said, but Abel was already moving.

He left the house and returned in under two minutes, which to Cain's mind was cutting it fine.

Abel opened the bag and took out a white forensic suit. He hurriedly stepped into it, then took their bag into the kitchen and remained there.

When Donald came back down, Cain was still sitting on the couch.

'Are you ready to go?' he asked Cain.

Cain stood up and put a hand on his chest. 'Do you think I could have a small glass of milk, please? I have horrendous heartburn. I've been up –'

'Of course. Through to the kitchen.' Donald started walking in that direction.

Well, that was fucking rude, Cain said to himself. *I wasn't even finished talking. I hate that, when some bastard interrupts me.* He silently took the latex gloves from his pocket and slipped them on.

He followed Donald into the kitchen, where the man opened the fridge door and bent down to grab a carton of milk. When he stood up, Abel, who had been hiding behind the door, stepped forward with the belt he had brought out of the bag and hooked it over Donald's head, pulling him backwards.

Donald let go of the milk carton and it fell to the floor, but it was still sealed and didn't leak. He struggled and tried to shout, but the belt was choking him.

Abel dragged him out of the kitchen as Cain put the milk away.

Donald was roughly hauled back into the living room, still struggling, and he was pulled onto the couch.

'Stop struggling, or I'll kill you,' Abel said.

Donald stopped and started gasping for breath as the tension on the belt was released.

'Who are you?' he said, gasping like he'd just run a marathon.

'Never mind who we are. We're going to ask some questions, and you're going to answer.' Abel watched his brother quickly step into his own forensics suit and pull the hood up. He put on goggles and tossed a pair to Abel, who put them on.

At that point, Donald jumped up from the couch, ran across to the pool table, leaped on top of it and grabbed a pool cue.

'I don't know who you bastards are, but you'd better get the fuck out of my house before I beat the shite out of you.' He swung the pool cue back and forth as the two white-suited men stood looking at him, smiling.

'We just want to ask you a few questions,' Cain said. 'Then we'll leave.'

'That was all shite about somebody murdering Susan, wasn't it?'

Cain smiled. 'That bit was true, actually,' he said as he and his brother walked towards the table, each on opposite sides. 'It was him.' He nodded to Abel.

Donald let out a scream of rage and took a swing at Abel. The cue connected with the man's left arm, but while he was distracted, Cain picked up a ball and fired it hard at Donald's head. It bounced off his skull, and Abel grabbed his legs and pulled. Donald fell onto the table with a thump and lay winded for a second.

Cain brought out the knife and held it up for Donald to see. 'This has been a long time coming, Vincent. You've been walking around breathing God's fresh air for too long now. This is your day of reckoning.'

'I have money,' Donald grunted. 'You can have it all.'

Both Cain and Abel smiled.

'That's very kind. But it's not money we want; it's answers.'

Donald talked then, with a false hope that they would let him go. But the knife that was rammed into his chest told him otherwise. Blood spattered their white suits, but Cain kept on going. He was breathing hard when he was finished.

Abel jumped up onto the table, grabbed the pool cue and rammed it into Donald's eye. If the man was clinging on to life at that moment, his tenuous grasp surely weakened and he let go.

Abel snapped the pool cue, leaving a piece sticking out, then jumped down, rubbing his arm over the footprint he'd left.

'Don't forget our little parting gift,' Cain said. Abel grinned as he went over to the bag and brought out the dead crow. It was wrapped in a polythene bag. He took the bird out and placed it on Donald's chest.

'There,' Abel said. 'Nobody will figure this one out. But at least we know what it means.' He put the polythene bag into the holdall.

Then he looked at the wall. 'Take a look at that, in the frame.' Abel walked over and had a closer look. 'Well, I'll be fucked.'

He took the frame off the wall, opened the back and took the picture out. It wasn't a normal picture, but a photo blown up and made into a jigsaw.

Cain walked over and pointed. 'Look at them.' He tutted. 'Break it apart and put that piece in his hand. That'll fuck them up. They'll be scratching their heads over this, let me tell you.'

The jigsaw had been kept together with spray glue and was easy to break into pieces. Abel took the piece that his brother had pointed to and put it in the dead man's hand. Then he broke the picture into more pieces so he could fit it in the bag.

'Let's get changed and get out of here,' Cain said.

And that was what they did.

'Who are we going to visit next?' Abel said.

Cain was still looking out of the window, at the hills, at the snow, but was seeing nothing. The pictures in his head were a different thing altogether. In another place, he was seeing what was going to happen and he was enjoying every minute of it. Not since they had served in the military had Cain been this excited.

'Did you hear me?' Abel asked.

Cain gave the knife a final rinse, watching the last of Vincent Donald go down the drain with the water. 'I heard you. I was thinking. We need to hit them hard. Fast and hard, just like the military.' He turned and looked at his brother, who was standing there grinning.

'I like the sound of that.'

Cain dried his knife and laid it on the counter. 'We go out again tonight. If we're lucky, the others won't have heard about our dead friend yet. If they have, then too bad. We're professionals, brother, and nothing will get in our way.'

'What about the polis?'

'Not even them.'

NINE

When they got close to Springfield train station, Craig was convinced they were well lost. They went under a narrow railway bridge, turned left and there it was, the station. Craig hadn't even known it existed.

'I should have just put it into the satnav,' he complained to Isla.

'I'm looking at a map on my phone. Keep going along here.' She looked at him and grinned. 'And I know you're itching to make some sexist comment about women and maps.'

'Who, me? I'm thinking no such thing.'

'Uh-huh,' Isla said, looking back down at her phone. 'Just up the road a bit.'

'You've said that three times.'

'This is the second time, cloth ears.' She shot a hand up to her mouth. 'Sorry, sir. I forgot I wasn't in the car with Dan. We rib each other like nothing on earth.'

'You'll be disciplined at the end of the day with a recommendation for demotion,' Craig answered, not looking at her.

'Oh God, sir, it was just a mistake.'

Craig laughed. 'Relax, Isla. I have to admit that's the first time one of my sergeants has called me cloth ears. My wife? I've lost count.'

'It won't happen again, I promise you.'

He laughed. 'It's fine. I'll let it go this time. At least you had the decency to pull a beamer.'

'I haven't!' She flipped down the sun visor and looked in the little mirror. 'Oh no. Please don't tell Dan!'

'Only if you buy me a pint on Saturday night when we gatecrash this do at The Dakota.'

'I will. I can drive you there and back so you can get proper sloshed.'

'No need. I'll just be having the one. In fact, I might even have a bottle of non-alcoholic.'

She flipped the visor up. 'Really?'

He nodded. 'Really.'

They approached a traffic light on the single-track road that went over the railway line.

'Talking of sloshed,' Isla said, 'what if they have a DJ there and they put on the Slosh? You game for that?'

'I don't think so.'

'Aw, come on, sir, it would be fun. Even though we'd be working, we'd be undercover, sort of.'

'No, we wouldn't. We'd be there to talk to Penelope Armstrong. Besides, these people are in their thirties, not forties like me.'

'I'm only just in my thirties and I'd be up for it.'

Something told Craig that Isla would be up for a lot of daft things. The Village People sprang to mind.

'Green light,' she said.

'That's another thing my wife does,' Craig said, moving forward.

'The Slosh?'

'Back-seat driving.'

'It's called co-piloting, thank you very much.'

'Two minutes ago, you said you weren't going to backchat and would treat me with respect.'

'Did I? I don't recall any such thing,' she said, grinning.

As detective sergeants went, Isla was one of the

better ones he'd worked with. A lot of them walked about like they had a poker shoved up their shirt. It was actually refreshing to have somebody with a sense of humour.

'You get on well with Dan,' he said, driving further along the road, waiting for Isla to suddenly shout, 'There it is, dozy bastard!'

'I do. And his wife. She's a sweetheart. I look on her as the older sister I didn't have. We go out on a Saturday sometimes, when she wants to lumber Dan with the shopping. He's such a gentle giant.'

'He was a good lad when we were in uniform together.'

'And he saved your life.'

'He'll never let that go. Not only twenty-five years ago, but a few weeks ago too. I'll never hear the end of it.'

'He's one of life's good blokes.'

The road went right through the golf course, now covered in snow, waiting for spring.

'Do golfers play golf in the snow, do you reckon?' Isla asked.

'How would they find the ball?'

She looked at him to see if he was taking the piss. 'They have yellow balls.'

'Would you be out there in this freezing cold?'

'Indeed I would not. But then I wouldn't be out in any weather pulling a huge handbag on wheels.'

'Golfers everywhere would be cringing right now if they could hear you.'

'Have you ever played golf, sir?'

'No. I've been into a few golf clubs in my time, but as for walking about on a green? I wouldn't even think about it unless I could take my Finn on it.'

'He'd have fun with the golf balls, right enough.'

The street they were looking for was called Drumwell.

'On the left, just at the "road narrows" sign,' Isla said, peering intently at her phone.

'Got it,' Craig replied, turning in. He was surprised at how well the roads had been ploughed. They started looking for the house numbers and Craig spotted the number 55 stuck to the side of a brick bungalow – modern, maybe twenty to thirty years old. There was a Mini on the driveway, parked next to a set of steps leading up to the doorway.

Craig parked, and he and Isla braved the chill wind. They were going up the steps when the door opened. That was something Craig hated, like every other copper in the land: go up to a door and have it open. There was no telling whether the person opening the door had a shotgun waiting or not.

The only threat was a beagle poking its head out, and it started to bark when it saw Craig approaching,

An older man appeared in the doorway. 'Missy, will you give it a rest?' he said, but Missy was having none of it. Barking and growling, she was eyeing up Craig like she wanted to hang off his bollocks and start swinging.

'Ladies first,' Craig said to Isla, stepping aside.

'Cannon fodder, more like,' she said. Then to Missy: 'Hello, gorgeous.' She put her hand down, and the dog sniffed her and wagged her tail. She gave Craig one last woof before turning and going back inside.

'That means she likes you,' the man said to them both, but Craig remained sceptical.

'Mr Renwick?' Isla asked, showing her warrant card. Craig held up his too.

'That's me,' the man said. 'Please, come away in.' He stood aside as the two officers came in.

'Take your boots off,' another voice demanded from further along the hallway.

Craig looked at the female; she was much younger than Renwick, perhaps a daughter or a girl-friend. Her blonde hair was wild, almost like Aimee Mann from her 'Til Tuesday days. She was wearing a dressing gown over pyjamas, pulling it tighter.

Her face was pale and waxy, her eyes dark and piercing.

'And close the bloody door,' she said. 'You're letting all the heat out.'

'I'm sorry, but we can't take our boots off in case we need to leave in a hurry,' Craig said.

She gritted her teeth and pointed at Renwick. 'You're cleaning up any mess, not me.' She turned and stormed away.

'Just ignore Kylie. She still hasn't got over losing her sister,' Renwick said. 'Neither have I, but I try to keep it together for her sake.'

'Can we come in and talk to you?' Craig asked.

'Aye, come away through to the living room. Can I get you a coffee or something?'

'We're fine, thanks,' Craig said, now taking the lead into the living room, in case there was another daftie sibling bouncing about. There wasn't. 'Can we have a seat?' he said, noticing that some snow had come off his boots onto the carpet.

Renwick was bald, and Craig couldn't tell if that was the way his hair had gone or if he shaved his head. His cheeks were rounded and decorated with surface blood vessels.

'Of course. Grab whatever you want.'

Craig and Isla sat on the settee, while Renwick

chose the seat that would seem to be the main TV-viewing chair as it was facing it almost directly.

Have you seen the news this morning?' Craig asked.

Renwick looked at him. 'Why? Is this about Susan? Did you get the bastard who ran her off the road?'

'No, we didn't get anybody, but what's happened does have a connection to your daughter. Vincent Donald's dead.'

What started off as a roller coaster of anger was quickly quashed. Renwick sucked in a breath and seemed to hold it for a record-breaking amount of time. Then he let it go in a whoosh and he started crying. Gentle sobs at first, then heavier crying, putting his head down between his knees. Finally, he stopped and looked at them, his eyes red.

'Can I get you something?' Isla asked. 'Glass of water or anything?'

The older man shook his head. 'Vince? Dead? How? Did somebody run him off the road too?'

'No,' Craig said. 'He was murdered in his house.'

Renwick looked at him. 'M...murdered? Oh God, no. Why would anybody murder Vince?'

'We were hoping you might have somebody in mind,' Isla said. 'Maybe somebody who had a grudge against your daughter or Vince that you didn't think about at the time of Susan's death.'

Renwick shook his head. 'I didn't think Susan's death was deliberate. I thought she'd been run off the road by a drunk driver.'

They heard shuffling feet on the carpet just outside the living room. 'I blame that bastard,' the daughter said.

'Kylie, that's enough!' Renwick said.

'Why don't you come in and give us your opinion, Kylie,' Craig said.

The young woman was chewing gum now, maybe in lieu of brushing her teeth or just to try to further enhance the hard-bitch persona she had been working on when they entered the house.

She took them up on their offer and came into the room. 'Susan would still be alive if she hadn't met him. She would still be living at home. I mean, he wasn't even going to marry her.'

'They were happy together, Kylie,' Renwick said. 'He provided her with a good home. Helped her with that business she started.'

'What business was that?' Craig asked.

'A consultancy. I don't remember all the details about it, but she was very happy.'

'Tell us about the night she died,' Isla said.

Renwick took a deep breath before speaking. 'Susan and Vince were going out for a meal at a wee place in Glenrothes. But I was feeling unwell. Susan insisted on coming over to check on me in person before going out. That's the kind of daughter she was.'

Kylie blew a bubble with her gum and tutted. 'I love you too, you know.'

'I know you do, love. I'm just saying that Susan loved me and your mother. After your mother died, she worried more, that's all. There's no inference there,' Renwick said, looking up at his daughter. Then he turned back to the officers. 'Anyway, she left to go and see Vince, and a few hours later, we got a knock at the door. It was two polis coming to tell me about the accident and that she was dead. Worst day of my life.'

'Were you at home that night?' Craig asked Kylie.

'Nope. I was out with friends.'

'Where were you in the early hours of this morning?' Craig asked, not wanting to skirt around the question anymore.

Kylie's mouth dropped open for a second. Maybe it was a family trait, Craig thought.

'How fucking dare you,' she replied, spitting the words out.

'It's just a process of elimination,' Isla said.

Kylie looked at her. 'Where were *you* last night? Both of you.' She now turned her attention to Craig. 'You look like a right glaikit bastard, with your beard that looks like it was in a competition with a fifteen-year-old's and lost. I've seen dead badgers that looked better than you. And now you come in here thinking we went round to Donald's house and killed the bastard? You don't get to come in here and ask those questions. You're in our home now, so you will fucking well answer *my* question: where were you last night?'

'We do get to ask those questions, actually,' Isla said. 'The Crown Office gives us permission.'

'Fuck the Crown Office. You see, this is how it could have gone down: one – or both – of you murdered Donald, and now to cover your tracks, you've come along to people who knew him and started throwing accusations.'

'They're doing nothing of the sort,' Renwick said to his daughter. 'Go and take one of your pills and calm down, for God's sake.'

'Pills? You think that's the answer? Don't be fooled by these two imposters.'

Craig sat and waited for the rant to die out, and when Kylie stopped to take a breath, he jumped in. 'Where were you then?' he asked again, calmly.

Kylie sputtered, as if a million words had entered her brain at one time and she was having trouble sorting them out.

Craig's phone dinged with a text, and he didn't bother excusing himself, but took the phone out and looked at the screen, making sure the others couldn't see it.

It was a photo from his dog-sitter. Finn was upside down on the couch, tongue lolling out the side of his mouth, rubbing his back from side to side. Eve called this his 'whacky doodle'; he loved to do it on the couch, or their bed, or his dog bed. Craig suppressed a smile.

Your boy's getting ready to go to the park. Ate his breakfast and he's pooped for the second time this morning. He insists I take him to a coffee shop. Smiley face.

Thank you, he quickly typed back. Karen was a godsend. They'd advertised for a dog walker, and she'd said she would take Finn all day. She was a writer, and as long as they didn't mind her writing while she looked after Finn, she would do it. They let her use the study and paid her well.

Craig looked at Kylie. 'That was the Crown Office. If we feel the need to get a search warrant, they can have one faxed through to the office in two minutes. I'll then have a dozen uniforms up here going through everything you have.'

'You wouldn't dare!' Kylie said.

Craig shrugged and made a show of looking at his phone again.

'Alright, alright,' Kylie said, holding up a hand, and running the other one through the rat's nest on her head that probably wouldn't look too bad with the aid of shampoo and a blowtorch. 'We were here last night, me and him.' She nodded towards her father.

'*Him* has a name,' Renwick said.

'Okay, I was here with radgie baws. That better?'

'Not what I was going for,' Renwick said under his breath.

'Anybody else vouch for that?' Isla asked.

'Yes, I had all the boys from the golf club round for a gang bang. I didn't get their names, though.'

'Kylie, for Christ's sake. You're just digging yourself a deeper hole here,' Renwick said, tutting and shaking his head.

Kylie sucked in a deep breath and closed her eyes for a second. 'Me and Pater here watched

Titanic. Not for the first time, either. Then we each went to our own room about...eleven-ish. And as you can see, I just got up. I didn't leave the house all night.' She looked at her father.

'I didn't either. And I liked Vince a lot; I wouldn't have wished him any harm.'

'You might want to talk to those losers he hung out with,' Kylie said.

'Who would that be?' Craig asked.

'The small group of people that he called his friends.'

'You have names for them?'

'Badger, Mason and Crystal. Those are their nicknames. When you catch up with them, you can ask the Crystal one how *she* got her nickname.' She mimed putting a glass up to her mouth and down. 'Bunch of snobby bastards.'

'Have you any idea how we can get hold of them?' Isla said.

'No idea.'

'Okay, thanks for that,' Craig said, and Kylie made a face like she would like to set fire to these people and eat them for dinner.

'As far as I'm concerned, Susan should have left the past in the past,' Kylie said.

'What do you mean?' Isla asked.

'She was Vince's girlfriend at university. They split up after uni finished. Our mum had just died and it was a rough time for us all. Then she bumped into him one night a few years ago. They got back together again. I wish she had met somebody else other than him.'

'Did Susan have a long-term relationship before bumping into Mr Donald?' Craig asked.

'There were a couple, but they both fizzled out. She lived on her own for a while, then she came back home,' Kylie said. 'Then she met Heid-the-Baw again, and after a little while, she moved into that godawful church he bought along the road.'

'Would you both consent to giving your DNA?' Isla asked.

'I suppose,' Kylie said. 'Give me the swab and I'll do it in the bathroom.'

Craig thought the woman would probably stick the swab up her arse if left to her own devices. 'That's not how it works.'

Kylie tutted and took the chewing gum out of her mouth and held on to it.

Isla did her thing with the swabs and packaged them up, then put them back in her pocket, while Kylie put the chewing gum back in her mouth.

Craig stood up beside Isla. 'If you think of

anything else that might help, please give me a call.' He handed over a business card to Renwick.

'I'll certainly do that.'

'I'm away back to bed,' Kylie said. 'The next time you knock on our door, make sure it's to tell us you caught the bastard who killed my sister.'

Alternatively, it will be with the drugs squad, Craig thought.

Kylie turned away and walked further into the house, and Renwick showed them out.

'She's highly strung,' he said, excusing his daughter's behaviour.

Outside, Craig and Isla got back into the car and Craig started it up. 'My gut says they're not involved,' he said.

'Mine too, but Kylie needs to rein it in a wee bit.'

'You heard her dad; she's on pills,' Craig said.

'The kind that would calm her down after a blackout, maybe?' Isla said.

Craig didn't know, but he thought it was a possibility. 'Maybe.' He took his phone out and showed her the photo of his dog upside down on the couch. 'It wasn't the Crown Office texting me, it was our dog-sitter.'

'Aww. He's a nice boy. Maybe Mr Boots would like him.'

'He could show Finn the new sweater he got for Christmas.'

'I get the feeling Finn didn't get one,' Isla said, shaking her head.

'He got a Santa hat, though. He doesn't like sweaters.'

'Cheapskate.'

TEN

Eve called and told Craig that Rose, her friend and colleague, had suggested they go for a coffee after work.

'You should go and have fun,' he told her.

'What are you going to do for dinner?'

'I'm a big boy. I can fend for myself. Karen's there with Finn until six, but if I'm running late, I'll pay her extra and buy her dinner. I mean, not take her to dinner but pay for her Chinese takeaway, obviously.'

Eve laughed. 'I knew what you meant. That would be great.'

'I just want to go and poke around our crime scene before I go home.'

'I won't be late.'

They said their goodbyes, and when he went into the incident room, he saw the others were getting ready to leave. He called Isla and Dan over.

'Did the warrant come through for Donald's house yet?'

'I have it on my desk, waiting for you,' Dan said.

'Right. I'll take it with me.'

'Are you going over there just now?' Isla asked.

'I am. There are uniforms there, so I won't be going in on my own.'

'Why don't I go with you?' Isla said. 'Mr Boots will be playing with himself just now. *By* himself,' she corrected when Dan sniggered.

'If you want.'

'Count me in too, boss,' Dan said. 'The girls will be doing their own thing and the wife is having a plastic tub party. In the middle of the week. I ask you.'

'Let's go then.'

Craig led them out to his car, and this time he knew where he was going. 'I want to see if we can find any information on those friends we found out about. Badger, Mason and Crystal.' He looked at Isla. 'The one with the drinking problem.'

He pulled into the side of the road outside the

school and could see the patrol car up ahead blocking the driveway to the crime scene.

'Still plenty of activity,' Isla said, spotting the forensics van.

'They'll be here for a while, so don't get in their way,' Craig said.

'As if.' Isla tutted and opened the back door and let the cold air rush in. They all stepped out of the warmth into the chill evening air.

Craig showed the patrol officer his warrant card and they went into the house.

Stan Mackay was still there, suited up. 'Hi, Jim. Dan. Isla. Anything I can help you with?'

'Hey, Stan,' Craig said. 'I'm looking for three names. They were friends of the victim's.'

They noticed Donald was long gone, leaving behind the blood-stained pool table.

'The news crew were round earlier. They have his name and no doubt there'll be a story about it on the news tonight,' Mackay said. 'But as for the names, the computers are already away to my lab. There might be an address book somewhere, but there's a lot of stuff around.'

'I don't suppose you found a jigsaw puzzle hiding in a cupboard or anything?' Dan asked.

'Nothing like that, I'm afraid. But please feel free

to have another rake about. With gloves on, of course.'

They split up, Craig taking the spiral staircase to the gallery level. More techs were up here. Craig nodded to one of them as he started going through the bedrooms again.

One of the bedrooms had a desk in it. Craig thought that the room had probably been built round this feature. An Apple keyboard sat on the desk, with a trackpad, in front of where the iMac had been earlier in the day.

He pulled a drawer open and saw it was a filing cabinet. Each hanging folder had a tab on it. He started flipping through each tab; they seemed to be labelled with the names of clients. He pulled a paper out and saw it was a bill for client services. Something to do with promotional material. It was obviously old, since the name at the top was Susan's and it was dated more than a year ago. This had been her office.

He pulled out a file that was labelled 'receipts' and rifled through it. There was an insert labelled 'Christmas'. He flipped it open and had a look inside. There were receipts for gifts she had bought Donald: some books, a sweater, a tie, a new tablet. The next one jumped out at him.

A receipt for a jigsaw puzzle.

ELEVEN

The next morning, Craig got up early, determined to maintain his routine, like he had done in London.

'Karen's fabulous with Finn,' Eve said.

Craig was slipping on his overcoat, and the dog came up and rubbed himself against his trousers. 'You like Karen, don't you?'

'She said she's writing a crime novel with a romantic twist,' Eve said.

'I wonder if she'll still sit with the boy when she's rich and famous?'

'Let's just thank our lucky stars that we have her just now.'

'I thought she would just come in and sit with the dog at lunchtime, but the fact that she can write here is fantastic.'

'What does her husband do again?'

'He's a manager at a DIY store. She does the dog-sitting for some extra cash. I don't think they're high-flyers, so this is perfect for her.' He patted the dog on the head and the Shepherd went back to his mum. 'See you later.'

'Are you picking Isla up?'

'No, she's here now. Leaving her car while I drive us over.'

Eve looked a bit pale.

'You okay, sweetheart?' he asked her.

'Just the thought of you going over to Edinburgh, and we're both going over there on Saturday to have that meeting with the doctors. I can't eat and I can't sleep.'

'You don't want to make yourself ill,' Craig said.

'Any more than I already am? Just take care.'

He kissed her on the cheek and went down-stairs. In this house the bedrooms were on the ground floor and the other rooms were upstairs; it had probably been designed that way so they would get a better view of the bridges across the water.

Outside, Isla was walking over to him, having parked her car in a little layby further up the road.

'Morning, boss.'

'Hi, Isla.' He indicated the Volvo. 'I've got the car running.'

'You're spoiling me.' She looked up at the window where Finn was standing with his front paws on the glass. 'Your boy's missing you already.'

'He'll forget about me as soon as Karen comes in.'

They got into the car.

'Karen's the new dog-sitter you were telling me about? How is she working out?'

'She great. She's writing a book, and Finn lies at her feet while she writes. She takes him to the park and then for a walk, but since it's so cold, just a short walk. Then he tells her when he needs to go out and pee by getting up and standing at the door, whining. She's done this before.'

'You had her checked out, didn't you?' Isla said, smiling.

'It's not like the old days when we could just nip into the system and put somebody's name through. That's a career-ender right there.'

'How did you do it then?'

'I have a friend down in London who's an ex-detective. He's a private investigator now. He ran her through the system.'

Isla laughed. 'And she came back clean or else

she wouldn't be in your house all day, raking through your drawers and eating all your food.'

'I hardly think she does that, but yes, she checked out.'

'I didn't mean literally raking through your skids drawer. I meant nicking the change off your bedside cabinet.'

They made small talk as they drove across the Queensferry Crossing and fell in with the hordes of people driving into work in Edinburgh.

Pamela Armstrong worked for the Caledonian Bank headquarters at Gogarburn. Craig took the slip road that crossed over the A8 and found a parking space near the front.

They walked into the building through a whipping wind and showed one of the guards their warrant cards.

'I'll give her a call, sir, if you could give me a minute.' He called up and then gave them directions to her office.

They took the lift up.

'I don't think I could work for a bank,' Craig said.

'It would be a lot less dangerous,' Isla said.

'I'd get bored. I like a little danger in my life.'

Pamela Armstrong was waiting for them in her

office. She stood up from behind her desk as Craig and Isla were shown in by a young man.

'Come in. I'm Pamela Armstrong. Is this about Vince?'

Craig closed the door. 'It is, yes.'

'Please sit down.'

Pamela was thirty-eight, according to her Facebook profile. She was slim, with short blonde hair and piercing green eyes.

They sat opposite her, Craig watching her face. Maybe she had done her grieving in private, or maybe she hadn't been grieving at all.

'What can I help you with?'

'How well did you know Vince?' Craig asked.

'We met at university. St Andrews. I'd known him for...well, we left fifteen years ago, went there for four, so almost twenty years.' She locked eyes with Craig. 'Have you got any leads on who murdered him?'

'Not yet. We wanted to ask you if you had any idea who might have wanted to harm Mr Donald.'

She sat back in her chair. 'I have absolutely no idea. He was a nice man, worked hard and gave a lot of money to charity. He worked with charities that help families who are less fortunate than we are. He helped a lot of kids over the years.'

Craig thought he heard something break in her voice then.

'What about two of his friends, Badger and Mason?' Isla asked.

Pamela's mouth opened and closed a couple of times before she cleared her throat. 'Who?'

'Oh come on,' Craig said. 'You're having a reunion on Saturday night. It says on your Facebook page that there's a lot of people going. I think you know Badger and Mason.'

She looked away for a second before making eye contact with him again. 'I'm sorry, I don't know anybody called Badger. That's a ridiculous name.'

'Did you keep in contact with Mr Donald after university?' Craig asked.

'No, not at all. That's why we're having this informal gathering. I've heard back from maybe twenty people who are interested in catching up. Mostly from The Crows.'

Craig stared at her for a moment, feeling the heat in the building getting to him after the cold outside. 'The Crows?'

She gave a small laugh. 'The rugby team were high-flyers. They were nicknamed The Eagles. The group of us who followed them to games was called

The Crows, because we couldn't make it as high as them. It was a joke on campus and it stuck.'

'And you haven't seen any of these "Crows" since university?' Isla said.

'I've bumped into one or two over the years, of course, but not recently. I thought it would be nice to get together.'

'You obviously kept up with what Mr Donald was doing,' Craig said.

'Only through the bank. Being a businessman, he gets loans through us. Got them, I should say.'

'Did you ever meet his girlfriend, Susan?'

'Yes. She was nice. I was sorry to hear about her passing a few weeks ago.' Pamela shook her head. 'Drunk drivers are all over the place. You can never tell when you're going to meet one.'

'That's true. And to have met one on a little back road in the middle of nowhere too. What were the chances?' Isla said.

They both watched as little round spots of red appeared on Pamela's cheeks.

'It was horrendous. Of course, you didn't get anybody for it, did you?'

'How do you know we didn't?' Craig asked.

Pamela shrugged like a sullen teenager. 'I just assumed.'

'We'd like to come along to the meeting on Saturday night,' Craig said.

'I cancelled it. I told everybody in the Facebook group that it would be in bad taste if we all got together just now.'

'Understandable.' Craig nodded to Isla and they stood up. And that was when he saw the photo in a frame on the wall. He walked over to it. 'This is Mr Donald, isn't it?' He tapped the glass.

Pamela got up from behind her desk like a rocket had been set off. 'Yes, that's him.' She put a polished fingernail below Donald's chin.

The photo was of a group of about twenty men and women sitting on stadium seating, the kind that was found in parks.

'Who are these people?' Craig asked, seeing a younger version of Pamela and putting his finger on the glass, pointing to her.

'Members of the rugby team, and some girl-friends. That's me, as you correctly spotted. That's Susan Renwick. Terry Bridger. This is April Chapman. And the last, beautiful man there is Lawrence Armstrong. The man who would later become my husband. God rest his soul.'

'He passed away?'

Pamela nodded. 'Four months ago. He was out

hiking and fell off the pathway, and a little branch went through his eye into his brain, killing him.' She took in a deep breath.

Craig nodded. 'Sorry for your loss. But let me ask you: are these players The Eagles?'

She gave a small laugh and then sniffed. 'Oh no. These were the duffers who couldn't piss in a straight line, far less kick a ball. These were The Crows. And we were their undying followers.'

'There was you and Lawrence. Vincent and Susan. Terry was with April?'

'Yes. Terry and April stayed together after uni, just like Lawrence and me. They got married a couple of years later.'

'Where do they live now?' Isla asked.

'Terry lives in Bowhill. His wife died last year.' Pamela looked at the detectives. 'She was a drinker. She liked to have a drink in the bath. She was drunk one night in the bath and slipped under the water. Terry found her dead when he came back from the pub.'

'Where was this photo taken?'

'In a park in Pitlochry. They have a rugby pitch there. Well, they did fifteen years ago. I don't know about now.'

'How many of these people in the photo did you invite along on Saturday night?'

'Just a few. The other people coming were from uni but weren't with the rugby team.'

'Do you mind if I take a photo of this photo?' Craig asked.

'No, go right ahead. It's actually a jigsaw puzzle.'

Craig looked closer, his nose almost touching the glass. 'So it is. That's a great idea.' He took his phone out and took a photo of it.

'Susan had it made up last summer, for my birthday. We met up once in a while, and she said she was going to give us all one.'

'Thank you for your help,' Craig said, 'and once again, I'm sorry for your loss.'

Downstairs, back in the car, Craig took his phone out again and looked at the photo he'd just taken. 'This looks exactly like the puzzle piece we took from Vince Donald's hand.'

'Who was on that jigsaw piece?'

'Him.' Craig held the phone out and pointed to Terry Bridger. 'I think that's the guy called Badger. I might be wrong, but it sounds like Bridger.'

'That would make sense.'

'I also think we were just talking to a woman who has the nickname Crystal.'

Just as he was pulling out of the car park, his phone rang.

'Boss, it's Dan. We just got a shout.'

'Whereabouts, Dan?' Craig said.

'Bowhill. Two victims.'

'We're on our way.' He hung up and looked at Isla. 'Bowhill?'

'Don't worry, I'll keep you right. Even if it means backseat driving.'

TWELVE

There was no parking in the cul-de-sac when Craig pulled in. There were too many patrol cars and other associated vehicles. A familiar-looking Audi was parked half on the pavement as if the driver had been pished and decided that off-roading was the way to go.

'Annie Keller beat us to it, I see,' Craig said, pointing to the pathologist's car.

'Yep, that's her style; if she can't find a space, she creates one.'

They stepped out of the car into the cold.

'Been a long time since I was in Cardenden,' he said, looking around. There were newer houses on the opposite side of the street, facing the council houses.

He locked the car and they walked under the crime scene tape, which was held up by a uniform.

Annie Keller was waiting outside the terraced house when they rounded the corner. She was wearing her white suit, but only halfway up. Her legs were in it, but the rest was tied round her waist. Her medical bag was at her feet.

Neighbours were gathering, shivering in the cold, eager to get a glimpse of whoever was dead inside.

'Is it Terry?' one of them asked Craig.

He ignored her, as did Isla.

'They all want to know, but they'll know nothing when we go knocking on their doors,' he said.

'It's the same wherever we go,' she replied.

'Detective Craig,' Annie said, pleased to see him. 'If I didn't know better, I'd think you were following me.'

'We have a mutual interest,' Craig said. 'Some people join a model train club; we have crime scenes. Whatever gets you out of bed in the morning.'

Annie laughed and looked around. 'Fuck it. I've been putting this off all morning. I was just about to skive off at the hospital and have a fly puff when I got the call. I'd been preparing my body for it, like a prize fighter preps himself for getting in the ring.

Then at the last minute, his opponent comes down with the flu, denying him the excitement of the fight. It's not right, Jimmy. I can't do that to my body. It's a finely tuned vessel. It's waiting for the roar of the crowd.'

'I'll try and hide you as best I can. Although Dan would be a better fit for this job.'

'Being a fat bastard?' she said, taking her cigarettes out.

'I heard that,' Dan said, coming across to them.

'A wee bit of a heads-up wouldn't have gone amiss, Jimmy,' Annie said to him. She popped a cigarette out of the packet and grinned at Dan. 'You know I love you, Dan. Like a brother, of course. Since you're...' She lit it and blew out smoke.

'Not your type?' he finished for her.

'Married,' she finished. 'I needed that.' She offered the pack to Isla.

'No thanks, Annie. I gave up for good years ago.'

'Wise choice, young lady. How about you, Jimmy?' Annie offered the pack to him.

'I never started, so there was nothing to give up.'

'Listen to him. Wee lamb. Nothing to give up. I'm sure there's more than one skeleton in your closet waiting to get invited out to the party.'

'If there is, I don't think I'll be introducing them to you, Annie.'

'I thought you were going to be the fun detective. Unlike DCI Mickey Thompson, God rest his soul. Fun Jimmy, that's the nickname I had in mind for you. It's going to go back to the committee for a rethink. But you don't want me to come back with the bad news it voted for Sourpuss Jimmy.'

'This from a woman who has too much fun cutting up bodies,' Dan said.

'We all have our vices, Dan. All of you included. And I'm determined to find out what your boss's vices are.' She took another drag, blew the smoke into the cold air and grinned at Craig. 'It's a work in progress, though.'

'You're going to have to work harder at it.'

'Give me time, Jimmy boy.'

'What have we got, Dan?' Craig asked, nodding towards the house where a uniform was standing guard and crime scene techs were bustling about.

'Two victims, both upstairs on the bed. Christ, it looks like an abattoir. Somebody went to town on them. You think seeing Vince Donald was bad, wait till you feast your eyes on this one. Even one of the crime scene lassies tossed her bag down the toilet. Fucking horrendous.'

'Uh-oh, looks like we're up,' Annie said, nipping her cigarette and putting it back in the packet. They turned to see the forensics photographer coming out, his face the same colour as his suit. Head team member Stan Mackay came out next, blowing air out of his puffed-up cheeks.

He walked over to them. 'Christ Almighty, I don't think I've seen such a mess in a very long time.'

'Bad, eh?' Dan said. 'That smell would give you the fucking boak. I rubbed some Vicks under my nose.'

'Let me borrow some, Dan,' Isla said.

'When I said, rubbed it under my nose, I was being polite. I actually stuck a finger up each nostril, just to make sure.'

'That's minging. Picking your bloody nose in public. Never giving us a thought.'

'You can have some if you want. I'm not promising the ointment is clean, though.'

'Remind me not to share my haemorrhoid cream with you next time you can't sit down.'

The others looked at her. 'Just kidding. I don't have haemorrhoids. I meant to say, share a joint with me.'

'Aye, aye,' Dan said, 'whatever you say.'

'I don't know what's worse,' Mackay said.

'Let's get inside,' Craig said, trying not to think of what might be in Dan's ointment jar or Isla's arse cream.

'Besides, I'm not old enough to get those things,' he heard her trying to convince Dan.

'That's just a myth,' Mackay said, leading the troops in.

'Thanks for that, Stan, but Annie will back me up, won't you, Annie? And she should know, being a doctor.'

'As opposed to me, who just wheeks a wee brush about a windowsill looking for prints?' Mackay said.

'Exactly! Tell him, Annie.'

'Well, they usually start at around age forty-five, but younger people *can* get them. Sorry, kiddo.'

'Next time you're pished and call me up at midnight on a Saturday night for a lift home, I won't answer,' Isla said.

'You don't mean that.'

'Try me.'

Annie tutted. 'Stan? I was wrong there. Haemorrhoids don't start until you reach sixty-five. Medically proven fact,' she said to his back. Then to Isla: 'There. That better?'

'Much.' Isla turned to Dan. 'See?'

Inside the house, the smell hit them first, even though the front door was wide open.

'That smell, along with the taster of what's to come from Stan and Dan, means all is not well chez Bridger,' Craig said.

'Upstairs,' Stan said, standing back to let them go up. Craig led the way, followed by Annie and Isla, with Dan doing the 'Devil takes the hindmost' bit.

The stench got worse as they got to the landing, and a white-suited tech there pointed to the room where the bodies were, like a tour guide showing them round the Manson house.

Craig stopped for a second, and Annie bumped into him.

'You should give a lady notice if you're going to suddenly stop,' she said. 'I mean, I might have been dreaming of George Clooney for a second, and there you have it, bubble burst.' She stood on tiptoes and looked over his shoulder. 'Oh dear, somebody had fun.'

There was blood everywhere, Craig saw, his eyes scanning the room. On the wallpaper, on the carpet, on the free-standing wardrobe. The chest of drawers hadn't dodged a bullet either. The ceiling too had received its fair share, and the light hadn't wanted to miss out on the action and had been sprayed as well.

Most of it was on the bed, though. The two blood donors were lying side by side on their backs, staring at the ceiling. Like they were looking to see if the killer had missed a spot.

He stepped further into the room, wishing somebody had told them to suit up. Annie put her bag down and pulled the rest of her white suit on, struggling a bit to get her right arm in. 'No, I've got it,' she said, leaning over like she had invented a new escape artist act and it had gone awry.

Craig turned round and helped her by holding the arm of the suit out straight for her until she got her arm in and stood upright again. 'Ta da,' she said, zipping it all the way up. 'And for my next trick, I'll need help from a member of the audience. You look like you would be able to help me, fine sir,' she said to Craig.

'I just did.'

'Don't spoil the illusion for the kids,' she said, nodding her head at Isla and Dan.

'If you think I'm going to stand here in my underpants eating an onion thinking it's an apple, you're sadly mistaken,' Craig said.

'I don't think our act is going to go far if you keep questioning my methods.' She opened her bag and took out a small probing tool which looked suspiciously like a crochet hook.

'You'll wake up one morning and find I've run away to join the circus,' Craig said.

'Thoughts of you being a clown ran through my mind there, Jimmy, I'm not going to lie. But you did open yourself up for it.'

'You did, sir,' Isla said.

Craig looked at her. 'Women stick together, obviously.'

Annie and Isla gave each other an air high-five.

'Jesus, this was personal,' Annie said, turning her attention to the victims on the bed. 'Somebody went to town.' She used the little hook to lift the man's shorts up. She had a quick look, then dropped them back down again. 'Just as I suspected by the amount of blood there, his testicles have been removed. And I mean, actually removed. The scrotum is there, but it's been opened up.'

'Mine just tightened up a little bit,' Dan said, voicing what Craig was thinking.

'That little nugget of information sent a shiver down my spine, I have to admit,' he said.

There was a lot of blood on the man's chest and neck. 'Multiple puncture wounds in the chest and neck, any one of which could have been the fatal wound,' Annie said, looking and probing.

The man's eyes were open and there were specks of blood on the eyeballs. 'The killer was still going at it when the victim was already dead,' Annie said.

'He wasn't just intent on killing him but annihilating him,' Craig said. Then he spotted the testicles sitting behind the bedside lamp on the man's side.

'There's his testicles there,' he said, pointing.

Annie looked behind her and stood up. 'It looks like they were placed there. I wonder why?'

Nobody could think of any reason why the man's bollocks would have been put on display.

Annie walked round the bed to the woman, who was naked. 'Stab wounds to the chest and neck also,' she said.

'Both killed in situ?' Craig asked.

Annie took her eyes off the woman and looked at him. 'Oh yes. The blood you see here came from them while they were on the bed.'

'Yet they're not tied up,' Craig said.

'What's the difference, sir?' Isla said. 'Maybe he was threatening them with the weapon.'

'I was just wondering: if somebody was lying there being stabbed, wouldn't the other one at least try to escape? I would. If, say, the female was being stabbed to death, and I was told to lie there and not move, I'd be off.'

'Maybe Bridger was frozen in fear,' Dan said.

'Possibly. Or maybe there was more than one killer. One on each side of the bed, threatening them with knives, say, and they were made to lie still. Then suddenly, there was a frenzied attack?'

The tech who had been standing out on the landing made to move past them, but Craig stopped him. 'When you took photos in here, were there any signs that the victims were tied up?'

'No, sir. That's how we found them.'

'Thanks.' He turned back into the room. 'Two killers is a possibility we have to look at.'

'That's why you're paid the big bucks,' Dan said.

'It's not that big.'

Annie looked at him. 'Said the sailor to the nun.'

Isla sniggered, and once again she and Annie did an air high-five.

It never failed to amaze Craig how he and the others could be at such a horrific scene yet make jokes. Any outsider would have been appalled, but it wasn't disrespect for the dead, it was a coping mechanism. It kept the nightmares at bay.

'Is there any way you can tell the time of death for them?' Craig asked.

'I'm going to say, within the last twelve hours,' Annie said.

'Thanks. We'll get out of here and head back to the station.'

'I'll call you later with my initial findings,' she said. 'Wait.' Annie bent over the male and opened his hand. 'Look at this.'

She held up a jigsaw puzzle piece by the edges. 'I don't know if you'll be able to get prints off it, but it shows a face.'

Craig went over to look at it. There was a man's face on it.

'Just like the last one. But no crow this time.' He turned to the others. 'Let's go and see if there's a jigsaw anywhere in the house. Catch you later, Annie.'

'Gotcha.'

Craig, Dan and Isla split up to check the rooms in the house. After a couple of minutes, Dan and Isla joined Craig in the living room.

'There's a frame there,' he said, pointing. It was leaning against the wall, just like in Vince Donald's house, and empty.

'Looks like they took the piece from there and took the rest,' Isla said. 'They don't want us to make the connection.'

'And yet we have,' Craig said. He looked at Dan. 'I'll tell you about it back at the station.'

Outside, Dan was whistling.

'What the hell are you whistling?' Craig asked.

'The Flintstones.'

'Why are you whistling that?'

'My oldest daughter's pregnant.'

'A lot of people play classical music to their unborn child. The wee yin will grow up thinking it's okay to go about in a battered old car with no floorboards.'

'I had a car like that.'

Craig shook his head. 'I think you're having me on. I think you just watch cartoons with your breakfast.'

'You got me.' Dan stopped whistling the theme to *The Flintstones* and started in on *Postman Pat*.

THIRTEEN

Abel was dancing around the living room like a swashbuckling pirate, poking the combat knife into the air, slicing and dicing with it.

'For fuck's sake, will you be careful with that thing?' Cain said to his brother.

'That's what she said,' Abel replied, laughing.

'I mean it. You'll have some bastard's eye out, and when I say somebody, I mean me. So put it away.'

Abel dropped the knife down and held it by his side. 'What if I was to take a benny and come at you with this?'

Cain tutted and shook his head. *Do we have to go through this again?* he thought. 'I would take it from you before you even got close to me, then I'd slit your fucking throat with it.'

'Hey, we were both in the military. We served side by side.'

'I'd still kick your arse.' Cain looked at Abel as if he really was going to come at him, but his brother merely turned and threw the knife at the living room wall, like a professional knife thrower. It hit the wall sideways and bounced back.

'I need more practice,' he said, walking over and picking up the knife.

'You need to stop doing that. Bloody idiot. I'm telling you, if that fucking thing hits me, you'll no' be able to walk for a week.'

Abel made a noise and walked over to the dresser where the sheath lay and put the knife inside. 'Just wait until I get a sword. That's going to be magic.'

Jesus, Cain thought, *that's all I need.* He sat at the small table in the living room and looked at his notebook. Things were going to plan. Last night had gone like clockwork, thanks to him. He sat back and ran it over in his head.

Badger Shaw didn't think of himself as a conman; he was just fast and loose with the truth. He was always dressed smartly when he went out: nice jacket, imitation expensive watch (he hated the term 'fake'), decent trousers and shoes that wouldn't pass muster at a country club but would fool a woman in a dark pub that had flashing lights.

Badger wasn't the best-looking bloke on the planet (by his own admission), but he had the gift of the gab, and he'd had some money. Thanks to his pal Vince, who himself had made a ton of cash with his stupid apps: he had invested his money and had shown Badger how to do it as well. Badger had made a lot of money. And lost all of it gambling.

This was the last thing he wanted to tell the woman he was standing at the bar with. Linda something-or-other. She was pretty and could hold a conversation. Just like his late wife could. He sucked in a breath for a moment, seeing April's smile, hearing her laugh, watching her walk and turn to look at him on the beach.

He couldn't believe she would be so stupid as to have a drink before getting in the bath. It was something she did every so often, even though Badger told her how dangerous it was. Then one evening when he was out at the pub with Vince, she'd had one too many and slipped under the water.

She loved to soak a face cloth and put it over her face, telling him it opened her pores. It was soothing and comfortable. It wasn't on her face when he found her dead. It was in the tub, floating around like it was laughing at her because it had just killed her.

But it wasn't the cloth of course. She had a high blood alcohol level, and had most likely fallen asleep in the warm water and drowned.

He had been inconsolable at first, but in the following four months, time had done its thing. He'd thought that was a cliché, but time really had helped to heal him.

Enough so that he was able to go out with women. Like this one. Linda something. He hadn't been paying attention to her when he had been ordering the drinks.

'...your place?'

He looked at her. Smiled. 'I'm sorry, what?'

'Are we going back to your place?'

'Of course. Let's drink up and get over.'

She smiled and finished her millionth martini, and Badger finished his beer. One thing Badger had always been good at was sleight of hand. She hadn't seen the powder he had popped into her drink.

Some of the women thought his house was a laugh. He could never tell if they would until he got them inside.

He was about to find out if Linda was amused by his gaff or not. But he knew by morning, she wouldn't even remember leaving the pub, never mind anything else.

'I was wondering if you were ever going to buy me a drink,' Linda said, putting her arm through his and pulling him closer.

'I thought you were with that other bloke – what's his name? Gordo.'

'Gordo?' She cackled in the cold, dark night, the sound seeming to reverberate around the deserted street. 'He's just somebody I've known for years. We're never been together.'

'Aye, I found that out later. That's why I bought you a drink.'

They turned into the cul-de-sac, Linda holding on ever tighter as the pavements were a bit slick.

When they got up to his door, he let them inside, neither of them paying attention to the Land Rover parked on the main road.

Cain had kept the engine off, and Abel was moaning about not being able to feel his bollocks anymore, and Cain told him he shouldn't be feeling his bollocks anyway.

'You're funny. But we could put the engine on for a wee bit.'

'It's a diesel. You would get more heat from a dead squirrel.'

'That's just making me feel hungry.'

Cain looked at him. 'How? Seriously, how the fuck does a dead squirrel make you feel hungry?'

'We've eaten worse on training.'

'That's true.' Then he nudged Abel. 'Keep down. Here's Charles and Camilla now.'

'Who?' Abel stayed down but was squinting through the windscreen.

'Our target. He's got a woman with him.'

'Oh crap. What do we do now?'

'I built this type of contingency into the plan.'

Abel smiled. 'Collateral damage.'

'Exactly, my friend. We remain focused on the objective, just like we were taught.'

They waited until the couple were inside before leaving the Land Rover, pulling their hoods up. Abel grabbed the backpack he had brought and slung it over one shoulder.

They walked across the street with their heads down, careful not to look at any of the houses in case they had security cameras, though Cain doubted they would round here.

They walked up to the front door and Cain knocked. They hadn't seen any lights come on downstairs, and he guessed that the couple had gone right up. There was no answer, so he knocked louder. After a few minutes, they saw a figure appear behind the frosted glass in the door.

Badger opened the door. Obviously, he was keeping it dark inside so nobody could see he was only wearing a dressing gown. Cain admired the man; he was a fast worker.

'Yes?' he said.

Cain held up his warrant card. 'DI Ross Naylor, Metropolitan Police.' Abel held up his too but didn't introduce himself.

'What is this about?'

'It's about your friend Vincent Donald. Can we come in and have a quick word?'

Badger looked behind him and then back at the two fake detectives. 'Look, I can talk to you tomorrow, but I'm busy right now.'

I'll bet you fucking are, Cain thought. Then Abel jumped in.

'We believe your life might be in danger, sir,' Abel said.

'What? Oh shite. You'd better come in then.' Badger stood back and let the two imposters cross the threshold and closed the door behind them. He was shivering a bit with the cold and leant against the radiator in the hallway.

Then Linda came downstairs, wearing a lady's bathrobe that had clearly belonged to Badger's deceased wife.

'What's going on?' she asked, and that was when Cain brought the gun out.

'Scream, and I'll shoot you in the fucking mouth,' he said.

Her mouth opened, but it was just to suck in air. Badger's mouth and eyes went wide.

'Are you married?' he asked his date for the night.

'They're nothing to do with me,' she said, barely getting the words out.

'Get upstairs, where you came from,' Cain said.

They both went upstairs, and back into the bedroom, where any thought of a romantic encounter was gone for the night.

'Look,' Badger said, 'I haven't got any money. I blew it all on gambling. This is a fucking council house and I'm six months behind on my rent. I don't have a penny to my name.'

'That's not what you said in the pub. You said you had a house in Spain,' Linda said. Then she looked at Cain. 'Does he owe you money? If he does, you can have him. Let me go and I won't say anything.'

'Strip and lie down on the bed,' Cain said, ignoring her offer. 'If you do as we say and lie quietly, we'll let you go. It's him we want.'

They both stripped and lay down naked on the bed. Abel walked out with the backpack and the couple lay quietly in the room, the only light coming from a small table lamp.

Two minutes later, Abel was back wearing his white protective suit. 'The bathroom's next door,' he said.

Cain left, giving his brother the gun. Another couple of minutes passed and then Cain came back, dressed the same. He was also holding two large knives. He passed one to his brother, who took it and put the gun down on top of a dresser.

'Look, why are you doing this?' Badger asked.

'Where is she?' Cain said, ignoring the question.

'What are you talking about?'

Cain felt himself go on fire inside, just like he had with the other one.

'Don't you lie to us. Tell us where she is.'

'Where who is?' Linda asked, sitting up. At that point it was all too much for Abel, who rammed his knife into her neck, slicing her artery. As he pulled the knife out, blood fired out in a jet.

Cain looked at Badger, who was staring at the maniac killing the woman. 'Where is she, Terry?'

'It wasn't me. I swear. It wasn't my idea. I left that night. I don't know where she is, honestly. If I knew, I would tell you.' He started crying, and then joined Linda in death as Cain plunged the knife into his chest.

'Are we going tonight?' Abel said.

'Tomorrow. I have some plans to work out. The next one is going to be tricky. We'll have to be a lot more careful. Let's just rest up today. Then we'll pay him a visit.'

Abel came over to his brother, who was still sitting at the table. 'Put your hand on the table, spread your fingers and I'll stab my knife between each of your fingers. Don't flinch.'

'Okay then, but if you miss and stab my hand, I'll cut your bollocks off, just like I did to Terry.'

Abel made a face. 'You're no fun.'

FOURTEEN

Davina was quite impressed by the young, professional female who had entered her house. Since her husband had been gone for almost ten years, it didn't matter that he wouldn't have approved. She had bandied about the idea of turning their home into a guest house after their kids moved out, but he had put his foot down. He wouldn't have strangers coming and going at all hours. He just wouldn't.

Then the stroke had come calling his name, and he'd died in a room with strangers coming and going at all hours.

Which left Davina with a hole in her life. Graham wasn't the world's best conversationalist, and the only company she'd had for many years was

The Archers on the radio. That and her plastic friend who lived in her bedside cabinet. She was sixty-four, not dead.

With Graham gone, she had longed for conversation, and after running it past their son and daughter (which was essentially an FYI), she had taken in lodgers. One at a time of course. She wasn't running a brothel, after all.

Of course, she had to do the laundry. But she only supplied breakfast. If she had served dinner, she may very well have gone tits up, as she heard one of her guests say one day. That had brought on one of her flushes, and she was glad when he was gone. He had been a crude man, an actor in a pantomime, and when it was finished, so was he.

The woman was standing in the room looking out of the window onto Cluny Drive.

'It's one of the better houses in Morningside,' Davina said, like she had to promote the room.

'I'll take it. I'll probably be here until the spring, while my house sells and I look for another one.'

'That's fine. At least it's only a ten-minute walk to the hospital from here.'

'That's why I chose it. I'm starting there tomorrow, but I have orientation today. This is so nice. And the en suite is so private.'

'I'm glad you like it. As I said on the phone, my terms are –'

The woman took her purse out of her bag and handed over an envelope with cash in it. 'That's for January. If you could furnish me with a receipt, that would be wonderful.'

'Of course. I'll be right back.'

'Please count it.'

'I trust you,' Davina said, leaving the room, and she had every intention of counting it.

Melissa looked out of the window and then at her watch. She'd better get a move on if she didn't want to be late.

She felt a shiver of excitement run through her. Quitting her job in Kirkcaldy and coming to work in Edinburgh was the best move she'd ever made.

FIFTEEN

Craig felt tired for some reason. This killer – or killers – was doing his napper in. He'd been hunting a killer in London who had been working like this. He had murdered a woman in her home and had left him a message, and then the next night, he had done the same thing. A psychologist Craig had spoken to had said this was very unusual, as serial killers usually took some down-time. But he had done the same on the third night.

Craig didn't think they were going to catch him, but by a stroke of luck, a taxi driver had seen him coming out of the third victim's house, and he knew the victim, knew she lived alone. Being a nosy bastard, he'd taken down the licence plate of the killer's car, and when he heard that his friend had been murdered, Craig got the call.

The killer was a bespectacled loner in his forties who was an accountant by day and a rapist by night. He'd worked his way up to killing women after raping them.

He hadn't put up a fight when Craig and his team had arrested him. He didn't deny it either.

Craig had a feeling that whoever had killed Vince Donald and Terry Bridger and his friend was a very different animal to the London rapist. These murders had all the hallmarks of professional hits.

He looked at Isla and Dan through his office window. Things were working well with them. And the others. Max was out with Jessie and Gary, interviewing witnesses, while the other two were setting up the board.

He lifted his phone and dialled the number he had written on a sticky note.

'DCI McNeil.'

'Harry! Jimmy Craig, Fife.'

'Oh hi, Jimmy. How are you settling in?'

'Thrown into the deep end, mate. Three murders in two days.'

'Jesus. What's happening over there?'

'They're linked. We're thinking that somebody's

got a list and he's going through it, taking people out for some reason.'

'Really? I wonder how big his list is.'

'One strange thing: there was a dead crow left at the first scene.'

'A dead crow?'

'Aye. The thing is, fifteen years ago, St Andrews University had a rugby team called The Crows. The main team were nicknamed The Eagles, but these guys were the ones who didn't make the cut but who still liked to play. This first victim was one of The Crows.'

'If there's anything I can help you with, give me a shout.'

'Actually, that's why I'm calling.'

'Fire away,' Harry said.

'I went through to Edinburgh this morning to talk to a woman in the Caledonian Bank. She told me her husband died when he went hiking and a small branch went through his eye. Is there any way you could run that through your system over there? It was in East Lothian.'

'Aye. Absolutely. What's his name?'

'Lawrence Armstrong. He died four months ago.'

'Let me look into it.'

'Thanks, Harry.'

'You coming over to Edinburgh any time soon? Maybe we could get a pint?'

'Absolutely. I'm coming over tomorrow to see Joe at the hospital. The doctor wants a word. Maybe we could catch up afterwards?'

'I'll be around. Just give me a call. Meantime, I'll look into that death for you.'

'Cheers, Harry.'

Craig hung up and went out into the incident room just as Max and the other two detectives came in. It was late afternoon now, and the day had dragged on. They were still collating information about Terry Bridger as well as looking further into Vince Donald's background.

'How did you get on with the witnesses?' Craig asked Max.

'We got lucky. Ish. A woman looked out of her window and saw a man walking about early this morning. He was wearing a hood, but she got a look at him: white, heavy built, looked young. He got into a dark Land Rover. She didn't know what kind, but she's seen them on TV. He drove away quietly.'

'He was alone?'

'Yes, he was.'

'There goes my theory that there were two of them.'

'Maybe he's clever, or fast enough to have killed them both,' Max said.

'Maybe he stabbed Bridger, say, in the neck or the heart, then killed the woman, and went back round the bed to finish Bridger off,' Craig said.

'That would work.'

Isla was putting up photos of the victims, sent over from the mortuary. Craig stood in front of the board, looking at the information she had put up. Including blow-ups of the jigsaw puzzle pieces after they'd been processed by forensics.

'The puzzle pieces match the framed jigsaw puzzle in Pamela Armstrong's office,' Isla said. 'DCI Craig took a photo of it and we compared them. The puzzle piece that was found in Vince Donald's hand shows Terry Bridger. The puzzle piece found in Bridger's hand shows another man from the photo. We don't know his identity, or why he was chosen. The others are connected because we think that Donald had three close friends, Badger, Mason and Crystal. We think that Badger is Terry Bridger. We don't know who Mason is. We think that Crystal is actually Mrs Armstrong, but she's not letting on if it is her.'

'Right now, we're pissing in the wind trying to find out who this Mason guy is,' Craig said. 'Max?

Maybe pay St Andrews a visit, see if they have any records of somebody called Mason.'

'Will do.'

'Go tomorrow. I don't want them rushing it because they want to get off home and they miss something.'

'Okay.'

'Dan, keep in touch with forensics and hurry Stan Mackay along for a result on the fingerprints. Although I suspect that if our guy was clever enough, he would have worn gloves. But keep at them anyway.'

'Right you are.'

'Tomorrow, let's see if we can find any business in Bowhill that has CCTV cameras outside. We might strike it lucky.'

After bandying some ideas about, they called it a day. Craig drove home to relieve Karen of her doggy duties.

'He's a real sweetheart. After he's had his exercise, he just lies down beside me, content to nap.'

'That's good. How's the book coming along?'

'I'm really excited about it. I have an editor lined up who's going to edit it when it's finished, and I have ideas for two more. Readers get excited when they find out it's a series.'

'Is your husband on board with you writing?'

She laughed. 'He says when I make it rich, he wants to retire. He's fifty. Can you believe that? I mean, it's not like I'm going to be the next Nora Roberts.'

'You never know.'

He showed her out, Finn following them, wagging his tail. Eve came in a little later.

'You look knackered,' he told her.

'I feel knackered,' she said.

'How were the kids?'

'First day back is always a circus, but at least it's only after their Christmas break and not after the summer break when none of them know what they're doing. I know how they were down in London, and it's just the same up here. They won't have much to do tomorrow since it's Friday and they'll be getting hyped up for the weekend.'

'Is everything okay?' Craig asked her, pouring her a glass of wine.

'I'm so nervous about seeing Joe on Saturday. I know you're going to see his psychiatrist at the hospital tomorrow, and we're both going in on Saturday, and I shouldn't be nervous, but I am. He's my boy, but I keep picturing him when he was arrested and that other personality of his came out. It was like he had been taken over and a stranger was talking to me.'

'That's what happens, Eve. Try and focus on the fact that that wasn't our son, but the other person living in his brain with him.'

'He killed people, Jim. He killed his biological mother.'

'She got into his head. Don't let that sway you; you're his mother.'

'Thank you. For everything. Sticking by my side, being there for me. I've cried a lot recently.'

'I'm always going to be by your side.'

Craig fell asleep in front of the TV after dinner, thinking of a little boy who'd called him 'Dad' and who would now happily put a knife through his heart.

SIXTEEN

Adam Langston sat in his office in the church, his iPad in front of him, looking at the woman he'd once slept with before he became a priest. It wasn't love at first sight, and she wasn't even his girlfriend, but back then they'd smoked weed and drunk until their eyes rolled back in their heads and it was a competition to see who could vomit the furthest.

Pam had won by the narrowest of margins. She had assured him that she and her boyfriend had split up, and although Lawrence Armstrong was pestering her to go out with him, she told Adam that she fancied him and that they should hook up. So they had.

He had been studying to be a lawyer, so they had given him the nickname Perry Mason, but after that night, *the* night, he had had a nervous breakdown and had ditched studying law to study Christ instead. The priesthood had been his only hope after that, and of course he had lied to get in. And they had accepted him and he had never looked back. He had never communicated with anybody other than Pam, Terry and Vince. Nobody knew his background except those three, and they were bonded together for life, after what had happened.

'I can't believe it, Pam,' Adam said, his Irish lilt becoming even more pronounced. 'Vince and now Terry. And they're saying that a woman Terry was with was also murdered. Who are these animals? Why us?' he said to the small screen.

Pamela Armstrong wiped her eyes. 'There's only one reason somebody would come after us, and you and I both know it.'

'I thought it was our secret?' Adam said.

'It is. Nobody said anything. I mean, we were all okay over Christmas. We had a good time.'

Adam took a deep breath and let it out slowly. 'I want to ask you something now, and don't go off your head: do you think Lawrence was murdered?'

Pamela sat back from the desk in her home office for a moment before leaning forward again. 'No. I don't think he was. I did a stupid thing, though.'

'What?' Adam was alarmed.

'I lied to the police.'

'Jesus and Mary, what did you say to them?'

'I told them he died on a hiking trail.'

Adam shook his head. 'For God's sake. It would be easy for them to find out he didn't.'

'I know that, but I panicked.'

Adam mentally shook his head. Fucking panicked indeed. Panic was reserved for when you thought you were going to shite yourself and the closer you got to the toilet, starting to undo your belt, the closer you were to letting go. That was panic. Or when you thought the johnny had burst when you were giving it the biscuit with a girl, the one who was the standby when you were pished but you would never marry in a million years. That was panic. Or when you thought the priesthood was going to be for the rest of your life, but you got drunk up in Fife over New Year's and slept with the woman you slept with at uni, and she was now on FaceTime telling you she had lied to the fucking police. That was definitely panic. But he kept calm, just like when he had farted when he was taking confession one day and hoped his parishioner, an older woman in her sixties, hadn't smelled it. (She had told her husband when she got out that she thought the priest was ill. And something about being pulled through with a Christmas tree.)

'You don't understand, Adam; they were like fucking Nazis. They were up my wazoo with all their fucking questions. They even asked about you.'

'Jesus, Mary and Joseph. What did you tell them?' He sat back a bit, almost like he was distancing himself from her. Pamela had always had a fucking penchant for exaggeration, and it was evident that she hadn't lost her touch after all this time.

'Don't worry, Adam, I didn't drop us in it. I told them I didn't know who Mason was.'

'They know my nickname?' *Aw, fuck me.* What else had she told them? That a priest over in Dunfermline smoked weed in his spare time, even though it was fucking medicinal? Same when he got blootered at the weekend. Medicinal. It wasn't easy standing for long periods with his bad back. Or sitting for long. He was up and down all the time like he had arse crabs, as his dearly departed (and not before fucking time, moaning old cow) mother would have said.

'They must have been talking to people near where Vince lived. Like the barman in that little pub or something. Maybe a neighbour,' Pamela said.

Adam shook his head. He should never have listened to the drunken cow at New Year's. *Let's go to the pub,* she said. *It'll be fun,* she said. And of course the nosy twat who ran the place had radar ears. They had stopped calling him Mason a long time ago, but Pam had shouted it across the bar. *Mason? You want a double?* He could still hear the echo of her voice bouncing around inside his head. He had made them promise they wouldn't mention he was a priest. *Tell them I'm a lawyer,* he'd said. *Tell them I'm a truck driver,* he'd said. *Tell them I'm Lord Lucan. Tell them anything but that I'm a man of the cloth.*

'If they're asking you who Mason is, then they don't have a clue,' he told Pamela.

He heard the words that had just come out of his mouth. They sounded hollow to him. Like when a dentist told you he was going to numb your gum, but you still felt the needle going in and a whistling pain shooting through your jaw the likes of which you'd never felt before and never wanted to feel again (though you knew that further down the line, thanks to your filthy sweetie-eating habit, you were going to). Hollow words, like those you'd say to a man on his deathbed, all soft and sugary, trying to put him at ease, but you knew it wasn't going to make a blind bit of difference.

'It's not the police I'm worried about, Adam; it's a killer who seems to know everything about us.'

And where would he have found out that informa-tion? he wanted to ask her. Maybe from some daft cow who had decided to organise a reunion without running it past their small group first. Not long after people had joined the group and started saying they would come along in January for the reunion, Terry's wife had died. April slid under the water in the bath. Tragic accident. They had sent their condolences and moved on with their lives. Only for Pamela's husband to die next. Then it was Susan, run off the road by a drunk driver.

That was the spouses, and now somebody was taking out the rest of the group.

'I want to tell you something,' he said to her.

'What's that?'

'I'm leaving the priesthood. I've had enough.'

Her eyes seemed to light up at that idea, like he was giving her an invitation to join him.

'That will be better for you. Will we still stay in touch?'

'Of course we will, Pamela, don't be silly.' *Why wouldn't I want you in my life? I mean, there's some nut job killing us because you had some fancy idea of getting together with a bunch of twats I didn't even like in the first place. With the exception of our little group.*

'Are you home just now?' he asked her.

'Yes, but I've put my house up on one of those short-term letting agencies. I have leave coming, so I told work my father was dying and I had to go be with him.'

'Didn't you already go to your father's funeral years ago?'

'Yes, but I didn't work for Caledonian at the time. They won't know the difference. Tonight, though, I've booked into a hotel.'

'Let's keep in touch, but through FaceTime only for the time being. It might come to us going our own ways, Pamela. Just for safety's sake.'

'I know. But let's not do anything we'll regret.'

Like getting pished and sleeping with each other? Too late for that, sister. 'Nope. Let's not do that. Call me at the weekend.'

'I will.'

Just then, her doorbell rang.

'Be careful, Pam!' Adam said.

'It's just food I ordered,' she replied, walking away from her laptop.

He watched her leave the living room, then he heard a commotion and suddenly Pamela was thrown back into the living room.

Then a strange man's face came right up to the camera.

'Hello, Adam,' the man said.

SEVENTEEN

Adam Langston recoiled, then swiped up on his iPad to disconnect the FaceTime call. *Who the hell was that?*

But he was kidding himself. He knew who it was: the man who had killed the others. It had to be.

Then he got a notification from his security camera, placed outside the church after a spate of vandalism. He opened the iPad again and tapped on the app. The view from the front of the church popped up and Adam saw a man in a hoody walking up the pathway towards the front door.

Christ, it was somebody coming for him. He closed the iPad again and rushed out of the office. He didn't have time to hide, so there was only one thing for it: go into the confessional booth.

He ran for it and got to the door just as the church door opened then closed again. Somebody was in the vestibule. The doors from there were open and he heard footsteps on the stone floor as the visitor came in.

He thought he had managed to close the door of the confessional without being seen, but the man's voice told him otherwise.

'Father, I'd like to make a confession,' the man said. He sounded young, and confident.

'Come in. Please take a seat,' Adam said, tightening his sphincter muscle.

The other door opened and the man came in. It was dark in here and Adam had a quick look through.

It couldn't be. It was the same man. How in God's name could that be? He had been talking to Pamela just now and he'd seen the man at her house. How could he be here as well?

Then a cold arrow shot into his heart as he realised: there were two of them.

'Go ahead, my son,' Adam said, making his voice sound normal. If it came out squeaky and girlie, then it was all over.

'I've done a bad thing, Father,' the man said.

Adam made sure to keep the little curtain divider mostly closed.

'Go on, my son, talk to me.' Adam slunk down a bit.

'Are you okay there, Father?'

'My apologies. I just noticed my shoelace is untied. Go ahead, I'm listening.'

While trying not to shite himself, Adam came up with a plan. He'd only have a few seconds to do it, but a few seconds was all that he was going to need. If he missed, he was dead, plain and simple.

As the man spoke, Adam kept down low and managed to get his own door open. A few seconds, he told himself. Light would come into the confessional, and if the other man was paying attention, then he would see it. Then it would be fifty-fifty. He had to risk it.

He opened the door. It didn't creak; he had made sure of that. Sometimes in the box it got hot, so he would gently open it a bit with his foot, but he didn't want to disturb his parishioners when he did that, so he made sure the hinges were always oiled.

He thanked the Lord above that they didn't squeak now. He was ducked down low, pushing the door.

'Did you hear what I said, Father?' the man asked, and that was the cue to move.

Adam grabbed one of the pews. Each row was made up of small pews, two bumped up to each other. The front ones were light, and not screwed to the floor, as sometimes they had to be moved to accommodate the choir singing; there wasn't much room between the front pews and the pulpit, so they were moved sideways out of the way. The ones behind were screwed to the floor.

Adam didn't pull the pew over but swung it round sideways and wedged it between the first screwed-down pew and the confessional box door. It wasn't quite an exact fit, but it was a couple of inches away from it. He grabbed the other pew and wedged it against his own door. It would take a Herculean effort to move them, so the only way out would be for the man to smash his way out. That would buy Adam some time.

His car was just outside and he had his car keys in his pocket. He sprinted up the aisle as the man realised he had been duped.

'You won't get far, Adam!' he shouted, and started kicking at the door.

Adam got outside into the freezing cold, taking

the keys from his pocket, and used the remote to open the door.

Unlike in a cheap movie, he had the door open and the engine going in a few seconds.

He fired out of the car park and didn't bother looking in the rear-view mirror.

EIGHTEEN

The young man slouched into the room, the grey hood of his hoody pulled up on his head, his hands dug deep into the pockets like he was cold.

'How are you feeling today, Joe?' Dr Shawn Solomon asked, sitting back in his chair, dispensing with his usual notepad and pen. He tended to do this with patients who had personality disorders. Even though there was an attendant standing just inside the door, he figured Joe could get to him, Solomon, faster than the attendant could get to Joe.

'Well, let's see, shall we? It's fucking Friday morning, and I've got one more day to work until the weekend, when I can go out and get pished. How does that sound?'

Solomon nodded. He wasn't talking to Joe just

then, but his alter ego, a man called Houdini. When Solomon had asked Joe who the other person inside him was, he had said the man's name was Houdini, because Joe had given him the challenge of escaping his brain. So far, this was one escape he couldn't pull off.

It was Houdini who had come out to greet Solomon this morning. It was a coin toss who it would be. Sometimes it would be Joe, because Houdini was tired and Houdini was having a lie in. Joe was scared to wake him, he said. Sometimes Houdini was dressed and ready to have a go at the world. Like today.

'Let me speak to Joe, Houdini.' Solomon had noticed that the alter ego didn't mind being called by this name.

Houdini chuckled. 'Now, why would I want to do that?'

'I'd like to talk to him. That's why I brought you both here.'

Houdini laughed. 'Pish. You want to talk about one thing: The Hammer. Isn't that right, Doctor?' He spat the last word out.

'How about you tell me about the killer, then? I mean, I can listen to you, but it would have been nice to hear Joe's side of the story.'

'Anything you want to hear, I can tell you. Alright?'

'Tell me then. Tell me why Joe started killing people.' Solomon looked at Houdini.

'You know why: James Craig. His father. Or should I say, the man who adopted him? Because that piece of shit isn't his father. Mickey was.'

'Mickey who?'

'DCI Mickey Thompson. He was having it away with that slut and she had Joe. "Oh, but I couldn't keep him."' He put two fists up at the sides of his eyes and moved them back and forth, imitating crying. 'Thompson could have done something about that. Kept it in his fucking pants, for a start. But Joe was born, and given away like a piece of fucking trash. Then he was bought by Craig.'

'Bought?' Solomon asked.

'Yes, bought! He adopted him and made sure he had everything he wanted.'

'Isn't that what a normal parent would do?'

'Yes, if you father one! But to swoop in and take somebody else's child is disgusting. Joe was angry growing up. He started to resent his father, the high-flying copper down in London who could do no wrong. Joe's head was spinning, but do you think his father had the time to sit down with him and ask him what direction his life should go in? Join the police, or mess around with computers, or something. Just sit down and have a conversation with him. The resentment grew.'

Houdini looked up at the ceiling for a moment. 'What's that? Oh right.' He looked back at Solomon. 'He wants me to tell you that he knew his father was working hard, but Joe needed time with his father, which he never got.'

'What about his mother?'

'Nice enough woman. Joe got on better with her than his father, but she was just as bad with the working. Long hours, coming home from being at school all day with other kids, marking homework and planning shite to do with the little bastards, when she had her own little bastard at home who needed her attention but wasn't getting it.'

'Is that why Joe sought out his biological mother?'

Houdini shot forward in his seat and the attendant was forward in a flash, almost touching his shoulder, but the doctor shook his head. The attendant stayed where he was behind Houdini without touching him.

'He sought her out because I fucking well told

him to.' He poked himself in the chest. 'Me! That was all me! Did he tell you otherwise?'

Solomon gave a slight smile. 'No. I assumed.'

'You know what they say about assume, don't you. It makes an ass out of you and me. Because that's what it spells out.'

'I won't make that mistake again. So tell me then, why did you want Joe to seek out his biological mother?'

Houdini sat back in his chair. 'Because that pair of fucks that he called his parents weren't interested in him. Weren't you just listening to me? I told him to seek out the mother who loved him. Just because she walked away, didn't mean that she didn't love him. I did that! I showed him.' He stared at Solomon.

'Was it his choice to kill?'

Houdini's head slumped forward and then slowly it raised again. 'Dr Solomon. When did I come here?'

Joe was back. The young man in his twenties who wouldn't hurt a fly, but who could be influenced by his other self.

'You don't remember coming here, Joe?' Solomon asked.

Joe realised there was somebody standing behind

him. He turned to look at the attendant. 'Oh hello, Mike!' He smiled.

'Hello, Joe.' Mike smiled back at him.

'Was there something you wanted to talk to me about today?' Joe asked Solomon.

'I just wanted to see how you were doing.'

'I'm doing fine. The medicine is helping me sleep better.'

'That's good. How are you feeling this morning?'

'A little tired, but I'm looking forward to watching some TV.'

Solomon nodded. The medication they were giving Joe was designed to take the edge off but still leave him able to speak to the doctor. It was a fine line, but he could see Joe was a well-turned-out young man. Or he would be if it weren't for the other personality inside his head.

'Can I go now?' Joe asked.

Solomon nodded. 'Yes, you can go. We can talk next week.'

Joe got up and smiled. 'Thank you, Doctor.'

Mike escorted Joe out of the office and back into the hallway.

As they entered his ward, a young nurse came up to him. 'Hello, Joe. I'm Melissa, your new nurse.'

'Where's my old one?'

'She left for a new job. Don't worry, Mike and I will take good care of you. Won't we, Mike?'

'Absolutely, Joe. You're in good hands now.'

They walked back to the secure unit, and Mike unlocked the door to Joe's room. They stepped inside.

'I feel so tired,' Joe said.

'You can get some rest,' Melissa said. 'You have to take some medication now, Joe. Mike has it. He'll give it to you. I'll go and get some water.'

Melissa left for a moment, and when she came back, Mike was standing with his back to her.

'Here you are, Joe,' he said. 'This will help you relax.'

Before Mike could hand Joe the tablets, Melissa jabbed him with a syringe, injecting him in the back of the leg. He didn't even have a chance to turn round before he hit the floor.

Melissa closed the door before anybody could see.

'Melissa?' Joe said. 'What's going on? I'm scared.'

'Never mind,' Melissa said. 'Get changed into his clothes. We don't have long. Then we can get the hell out of here.'

NINETEEN

Eve sat in her car and watched the northbound train stop at the station. 'It's times like these that I wish I smoked.'

'Just bite your fingernails like I do,' Craig said.

'Did you remember to buy your ticket?'

'I downloaded the app last night and bought it.'

'I wish you were driving,' Eve said.

'The parking's horrendous. I haven't been into Edinburgh for a long time. And yesterday doesn't count; that was on the outskirts. Besides, Harry McNeil said he would have somebody pick me up and drive me from Haymarket, and I can get a cab up to the hospital.'

'Call me when you've spoken to the doctor.' She

looked at the clock on the screen. 'Listen, I'd better shoot or I'll be late.'

'Okay. Drive safely.' He kissed her on the cheek and got out of the car, then watched her drive away before walking over to the southbound platform. He stood there, aware of his surroundings, but there wasn't anybody near him. He had already planned out how he would fight somebody if they tried to push him in front of the train, but nothing dramatic happened and he got on board safely with everybody else. Eve would have laughed at him, but he would have told her that nobody had managed to push him in front of a train so far. And he had never been mugged.

It was because he looked intimidating, she would say. This was also the reason nobody spoke to him at parties.

The ride over to Edinburgh went smoothly, and when he got off at Haymarket, he was careful not to be knocked down by one of the trams outside the train station.

An unmarked saloon car was parked just in front of the taxi rank opposite. There was a man in the front passenger seat and a younger woman behind the wheel. Harry McNeil had said he would send two officers up to meet Craig, DI Charlie Skellett and DS Lillian O'Shea.

Craig walked to the pedestrian crossing to get across, as the traffic was heavy and he didn't want to make an arse of himself by trying to run between the vehicles. Just one fall and he'd be a laughing stock. You could rescue five kids by yourself from a burning orphanage, but trip in front of your colleagues and you would forever be known as the dickhead who tripped in front of a bus.

The passenger window buzzed down as he got closer, and a small puff of cigar smoke came out and introduced itself to his nostrils.

'Medicinal,' Skellett said. 'I'm DI Charlie Skellett, sir. You can sit in the front if you give me a minute. I've got a messed-up knee and I wear a brace.'

'DCI Jim Craig. Pleased to meet you.' They shook hands, and Skellett made a show of fannying about with his walking stick.

'You stay there. I'll hop in the back.'

'Thanks.' Skellett buzzed up the window and Craig opened the back door and got in.

Lillian turned round and smiled at him. 'I'm DS O'Shea, but you can call me Lillian if you like. Or

DS O'Shea – whichever you prefer, sir.' She shook hands with him.

'What does everybody else call you?' Craig asked, noting the slight Irish accent.

'Leprechaun,' Skellett said.

'Lillian,' she corrected.

'Lillian it is. I'm a guest in your division, so I'll go with the flow.'

She started the car and pulled into traffic.

'DCI McNeil said you transferred up from London, sir,' Skellett said.

'Yes. Time for a change after twenty-five years. My wife transferred too. She's a teacher.'

Skellett sucked in a breath. 'Brave lady. I'd much rather be doing this job than dealing with those little bast...I mean, monsters. There's no discipline these days. Get away with murder, so they do. Not literally, but they think they're entitled, and when they grow up, we get to deal with them.'

'Charlie!' Lillian said. 'Not every kid is like that. It's not a reform school DCI Craig's wife works at, I'm sure.'

Craig laughed. 'He's got a point. Same down in London. Little bastards run riot. But you're right, my wife doesn't work at a reform school, if there's any such thing anymore.'

'She must have the patience of a saint,' Lillian said.

'She drinks wine at the weekend.'

Skellett laughed. 'Mine too. And given half the chance, so would my dog, Sir Hugo. He's a bulldog and I love him to bits. Mind you, the wife's a close second, so it's all good.'

Craig and Skellett swapped stories about their dogs, each man feeling a new respect for the other even though they'd only known each other for a few minutes.

Craig was lost as Lillian navigated her way through streets that had changed a great deal since he had last been here. When he and Eve had come up for a visit, they would come over for a night out, but they always took the train and didn't drive here, so he was completely lost.

After fifteen minutes, with Charlie Skellett going into great detail about how his dog loved his Sunday roast, Lillian pulled into the car park at Fettes Station down in Comely Bank, a leafy suburb where house prices had gone through the roof recently.

'You got any pets, Lillian?' Craig asked as they got out of the car.

'I've been out with a few animals in my time, but

never owned a pet.'

'Amen to that,' Skellett said, struggling out of the car. Craig grabbed his arm but saw it was only making things worse, and he didn't want the older man to take a heider because he'd cocked up helping him, so he let go and stepped back, ready to grab him if he overbalanced, but he made it out in one piece.

'Before I was married,' Skellett said, carrying on the conversation as if there hadn't been a break in between, 'I used to go into town with my muckers. Some of the states we saw: young lassies wearing skirts that were so short they should have been classified as belts, tossing their bag in the street. It would bring tears to a grown man's eye, so it would. I don't envy young men going up to those places nowadays.' He slammed the passenger door shut.

'Is that shut?' Lillian asked sarcastically.

'Aye,' Skellett answered. 'Besides, it's no' yours.'

'Fair dos.'

Skellett hobbled across the car park with Craig and Lillian. The wind cut through them.

'You been married a long time, sir?' Skellett asked Craig.

'We met in high school and we've been together ever since.'

'Impressive.' Skellett talked about how he

169

thought young people weren't in it for the long haul nowadays, and Lillian disagreed.

'Coffee, sir?' Lillian said when they were inside.

'Aye, that would be great.' Craig took his wallet out and handed over some money. 'Get yourself one for going.'

She laughed and started walking away.

'Oh, what about Harry and the others?' Craig asked.

'They know where the canteen is, don't worry.'

Skellett took Craig into the incident room. Some of the other members of Harry's team were busy at their computers. 'That's Harry's office over there. And the other one belongs to –'

Before he had a chance to finish, the other door opened and DSup Calvin Stewart walked out.

'Charlie! There you are. I hope you're not bending that laddie's fucking ear?'

'Just promoting the attractions that Edinburgh has to offer, sir.'

'Bollocks. Was he talking about his fucking dug again?'

'We shared stories about our dogs, yes.'

'DCI Jim Craig, this is DSup Calvin Stewart,' Skellett said.

'Pleased to meet you, sir,' Craig said.

'Likewise, son.' They shook hands.

Stewart was a big man who took nonsense off nobody. He turned to Skellett. 'I hope you weren't smoking those smelly wee cigar things in the car again.'

'Wouldn't dream of it. And the technical name for them is "cheroots". And they're medicinal for my leg pain.'

'Don't talk shite.' To Craig: 'Did you see smoke in the car?'

'I didn't. And I think I have a cold coming on, so my sense of smell isn't up to snuff.' It wasn't a lie; Craig had seen the smoke when it was already outside of the car.

'It just needs one of those drug-sniffing dugs to go off its heid near that car and I'll know you're a lying bastard,' Stewart said to Skellett.

The other office door opened, and DCI Harry McNeil came out.

'Here's your guest, Harry, son,' Stewart said.

'Jimmy, glad you could make it over,' Harry said.

'Glad to be here, but I wish it was more of a social visit.'

'Maybe we could combine both.'

'The laddie's here to work, no' get pished,' Stewart said.

Lillian came back in with Craig's coffee and his change.

'Thanks, Lillian,' he said.

'No problem, sir.'

Harry said, 'Come away into the office. I have that information you were asking about.'

Craig followed him in, sipping the coffee through the hole in the lid.

'Grab a pew, Jimmy,' Harry said.

'Cheers.'

'Never lost your accent, I see,' Harry said, sitting down in his chair.

'Neither did my wife. We're both Fifers, and it's like we never left.'

Harry grabbed a buff folder from one of the trays on his desk. 'Have a wee look through that. It'll surprise you.'

Craig put his coffee on the desk and took the offered file and set it down, opening it. He read through the report into Lawrence Armstrong's death.

When he was finished, he looked at Harry. 'His widow, Pamela, told us he'd died hiking.'

'There might have been some exercise going on, but it wasn't on a trail.'

Lawrence Armstrong had been found dead in a hotel, apparently of an overdose.

'Fentanyl in the cocaine. She never mentioned her husband was a junkie,' Craig said. 'I wonder why she lied?'

'Probably because she's some kind of manager at the bank and didn't want it to look bad to her colleagues.'

'Maybe she's lived with the lie about him hiking for the four months since his death and it's started to seem like the truth,' Craig said. 'Interesting that there was women's underwear there. Plus a woman made the treble-nine call. Could have been a prossie.'

'Or he was just messing about on his wife. Either way, we haven't traced the woman. Not back then, not now.'

'What kind of hotel is it?'

'The Kensington is middle of the road. Not a complete crap hole, but they turn a blind eye.'

'I should maybe go and talk to Pamela again. If you want to jump on board?'

'Absolutely. Do you want to call ahead and let her know we're coming?'

'I'll do that now.' Craig took his phone out and Harry left the office.

When he got through to the bank and identified himself, Craig was told that Pamela Armstrong was on leave. He asked for her address and waited for the details. He wrote the address on a piece of paper, thanked the woman and stood up. Taking his coffee – which was surprisingly good – he went into the incident room.

'How's the coffee?' Lillian asked him, smiling.

'It's pretty good, actually.'

'How long are you here for, son?' Stewart asked.

Craig wasn't sure if the DSup meant for the day or what.

'I heard you were up from London,' Stewart elaborated.

'Oh. I transferred from London to Fife.'

'By choice?'

'Aye. The wife and I decided to move up here.' Craig looked at Stewart. 'Can I have a word in DCI McNeil's office, sir?'

Stewart stood up straight, expecting trouble from the younger DCI. 'Let's go.'

As Craig closed the door, the two men stood facing each other, as if they were going to start boxing, but Craig merely sipped his coffee.

'I don't know if you've heard, but today I'm going to visit my son, Joe, in the Royal Edinburgh. Joe is in there being assessed. He's accused of being a serial killer.'

'Jesus, I did hear about that case, right enough. Sorry to hear that, son. If you need anybody's help here, call me directly. When I kick somebody's arse, I take names, if you know what I mean. Nobody will fuck with you in here.'

'I appreciate that. Everybody has been supportive, including my own crew, but I wanted to be upfront with you.'

'That couldn't have been easy, so I appreciate that. Nobody in here will treat you any differently. They're a good bunch. Don't tell them I said that.'

'Your secret's safe with me.'

They went back out to the incident room and Harry was waiting.

'You got the address?' he asked.

'I have. I'm not sure where it is. Succoth Place,' Craig said.

Harry looked at the address on the piece of paper. 'Murrayfield. I live up that way. We're practically neighbours. Come on, I know where that is. Two minutes up the road.'

They went out to Harry's car, Craig pulling his collar up against the cold wind.

'How are you finding the weather?' Harry said as they got into his car.

'We used to visit and it wasn't too bad, but now

I'm living up here again, I realise I'd forgotten how cold it gets.'

The house was on a side street, not far from where Harry said he lived. It was semi-detached, a big stone place with two levels.

'Must be worth a fortune,' Craig said as they got out and walked up the front pathway.

'She works in the bank, you said. She probably gets a cheap mortgage.'

Craig noticed it first: the front door was slightly ajar. He looked at Harry and nodded. *Prepare yourself.* He knocked on the door, pushing it inwards as he did so.

'Hello? Mrs Armstrong? It's DCIs Craig and McNeil.' He stepped into the vestibule. Another door faced them and it too was ajar. Craig pushed this one too.

'Mrs Armstrong? Police!' he shouted. There was no answer.

They both saw the things strewn around on the floor.

'I'll check upstairs,' Harry said and made his way up. Craig walked into the living room on the left and saw everything had been scattered around. He was looking through all the stuff when Harry came back in.

'Nothing amiss upstairs,' he said.

'Look at this,' Craig said. He nodded to a photo frame on the floor with smashed glass. The photo was the same one that had been made into a jigsaw puzzle.

'What is it?'

Craig looked at him. 'This is a photo of a group of friends taken in Pitlochry.'

'When?'

'I'm not sure. Pamela was at university fifteen years ago, at the end of her stint.' He pulled on a pair of latex gloves and carefully removed the photo from the frame. He turned it over, thinking that maybe a date had been written on it.

There was more than that. It put names to faces.

He took his phone out and took a photo of the back and front.

'I'll call this in,' Harry said.

Then Craig got a call. It was the hospital.

TWENTY

'What are you going to do?' Pamela screamed. 'Rape me and murder me?'

Cain came into his living room, running a hand through his hair. He yawned and stretched. He was dressed only in his boxers and vest.

'What's fucking going on?' he said, his eyes narrowing.

'I just took the gag out,' Abel said. 'I told her not to shout or scream, but she's non-stop.'

Cain walked forward and grabbed hold of her face between his thumb and fingers. 'Now, you listen to me, Princess: you need to shut your fucking hole. We don't want to kill you, just like we didn't want to kill the others, but they made us.'

'They made you kill them?' Pamela said after he let her face go.

'Yes. They wouldn't tell us what we wanted to know. Despite us torturing them, they didn't tell us. Now it's your turn.'

'I want breakfast,' she said.

'Really? You want me to nip out to McDonald's?'

'That would be nice.'

'Tough. There isn't one for miles around. In fact, there's *nothing* for miles around.'

'Where are we?' she asked in a quieter voice.

'Back where it all started, sweetheart.'

'Back where what started?'

'Don't act all innocent, Pamela. You're the one who got this ball rolling, you and your little reunion.'

'You kidnapped me because of a reunion between some uni friends who last saw each other fifteen years ago? That doesn't even make sense.'

'You know what you did,' Abel said, still holding the gag as if he was going to jump forward and tie it on again.

'I really don't.'

'Your husband understood. He didn't have the answers, though.'

Her jaw dropped down. 'So you killed him?'

Abel laughed. 'It was easy. He took a whore to

that dive hotel and she was already three sheets to the wind. Did you know your husband was a junkie?'

'I know he smoked weed when we were at uni.'

'He progressed to the big stuff,' Cain said. 'Cocaine. He went to the hotel to snort it with that whore. They would be jacked up before they went at it. We went in as waiters and she let us in. Abel here opened the champagne and popped in some roofies. Neither of them knew what had happened to them. We decided to let her go, so she left, bouncing all over the place. Then we went to town on your husband.'

'What do you mean, *went to town*?' Pamela asked.

'You know, we tried a different approach with Lawrence. We tried threatening him: we told him we would rape you. Which we wouldn't, of course; we're not fucking animals.'

'Not animals? Look what you did to Vince.'

'Now you're interrupting me.' Cain tutted and shook his head. 'And you know what Vince told us? He told us that you and that pervy fucking priest knew where she is.'

'What do you mean, pervy priest?' she said, her voice going quieter.

'You slept with him back at uni. Adam Langston, in case I was confusing you.'

'We all slept around at one point or another.'

'But Adam was your boyfriend,' Abel said, nodding towards Cain, as if he had just revealed some great secret. Cain silenced him with a look.

'Adam was the one you really wanted to be with, according to Lawrence. He had been your boyfriend before you were introduced to Lawrence, who wouldn't take no for an answer. He got his own way in the end. What happened, Pam?'

She looked at Cain, not saying a word.

He walked over to the cabinet and took Abel's knife out of the sheath and calmly walked back over to Pamela. To give the woman her due, he thought, she wasn't struggling against the ropes that were holding her fast to the chair.

'I don't know what you want from me.'

Cain held up the knife for her to see. 'Just tell us your version of what happened that night. We just want to find her. We've waited a long time.'

TWENTY-ONE

Traffic was chaotic in Morningside when Craig and Harry got there, but the car's sirens and blue flashers behind the grille got them through.

'How in the name of Christ could this have happened?' Craig said for the millionth time.

'Somebody's head's going to roll for this,' Harry said.

He turned into the car park of the not-quite-secure hospital. There were police patrol vehicles parked at either end of the car park as if all the patients were about to make a break for it.

They parked at the front and got out, and were escorted inside, where some of Harry's team were waiting.

'We need everything you've got on this woman

who walked out with your son, Jimmy,' Calvin Stewart said.

'It isn't a lot,' Craig said.

'Jimmy, this is DI Frank Miller,' Harry said, introducing them.

'Sir,' Miller said, nodding.

'Frank.'

'DS O'Shea and DC Colin Presley are upstairs talking to the staff.'

'We call Colin "Elvis",' Harry said.

'Naturally.'

'I just got here,' Stewart said, 'so let's get upstairs and find out what fucking twat's getting his jotters first.' He looked at the uniforms guarding the door. 'You two, if Lord Lucan and Jimmy Hoffa come down asking to go outside for a fag, they're probably imposters.'

'Yes, sir.' Craig saw one of them look at the other and mouth, *'Who's Jimmy Hoffa?'*

Upstairs, there was a sense of unrest as the attendants tried to keep the patients calm. Craig saw one man standing talking to staff members, and waited until he came over.

'DCI Craig,' Dr Shawn Solomon said, coming across to them and stopping.

'Doctor.'

Stewart looked at the doctor. 'You want to tell us how the fuck one of your patients just waltzed out of here? And don't give us the edited version.'

Solomon looked at him. 'I can sense an underlying current of anger running through you. Would you like to make an appointment to come and see me some other time?'

'Don't try your fucking psychobabble on me, you jumped up little twat. The chances of you having a job tomorrow are slim to none, so get on with it and tell us the point where your career was washed up.'

'Who are you?' Solomon said, turning his nose up at Stewart. Then to Craig: 'Do you know this man?'

'Detective Superintendent Stewart.'

'That's me,' Stewart said. 'Tell us how a psychopathic killer just walked out with one of your nurses. I mean, that is right, isn't it? I did hear my sergeant correctly when the call came in? Walked out. Nobody tried to stop them, and now they're in the wind.'

'It was a bit more involved than that.'

'Really? I'm all fucking ears.'

Solomon took a deep breath and let it out. 'We hired a new nurse to work on Joe's ward, apparently. I didn't do the hiring, obviously, but she seemed pleasant enough. This was her first day, after she did orientation. Mike was Joe's attendant, and he walked Joe back to his room with the new hire. Melissa something; I don't know her last name. We don't know quite what happened after that, but Mike was injected with something and it knocked him out. He's about the same size as Joe, so they dressed Joe in Mike's clothes and vice versa, and when somebody checked in on Joe, it was really Mike with the hoody on, sound asleep, facing away from the door.'

'Who discovered him?' Harry asked.

'One of the other nurses went in with Joe's meds and discovered Mike drooling out of one side of his mouth. We suspect he was given ketamine.'

'And you're sure that this woman took my son out of the hospital?' Craig asked.

'Yes. She kept her head down going out of the hospital, but it's not as if we couldn't identify her: dark hair, plump, Irish.'

'Irish?' Craig said.

'Yes.'

Craig tried to think if he knew any Irish woman who Joe might have known. If he did indeed know her.

'How did he react to her?' Craig asked.

'He was fine with her,' Solomon said. 'Like he

was fine with me. Like he was fine with his attendants. Like he would have been fine with canteen staff.' Solomon was starting to lose it, Craig saw, and he took him to one side.

'Nobody's blaming you for this,' he said to the doctor. 'Whoever this woman is, she took Joe for a reason. Let's get our heads together and try and find my son. I know he's dangerous, but he didn't walk out of here of his own volition. Somebody took him and I want to know why.' He put a hand on Solomon's shoulder.

'Who's that bloody maniac?' Solomon whispered, talking about Stewart

'That's who they send in when everything else has failed.'

'He's early.'

'Don't let him get under your skin. And for God's sake, don't annoy him.'

'Way ahead of you.'

'Get somebody to get them,' Stewart said. Then to Solomon: 'Where are the offices?'

'In the old building across the way.'

'Well, don't just stand there, ya glaikit bastard, get on the phone.'

CHAER 22

'Melissa Thompson, aged twenty-eight,' Harry said as they parked at the end of the street. They were stopping traffic at either end of Cluny Gardens and the side streets so nothing was coming along. Anybody looking out of their house window would maybe wonder why there was suddenly no traffic, so they had to move quickly. Armed officers would lead the charge and uniforms would be in the background, ready to tell neighbours to stay inside.

As plans went, it wasn't the best, but it was all they had at such short notice.

'They're going in now. The house is surrounded,' an anonymous voice said over the radio.

Then the units pulled in at high speed, and it went like clockwork: the door was taken off its hinges and men with machine guns who weren't pissing about entered the house.

Harry McNeil waited for the order that it was all clear, before he, Calvin Stewart and Lillian entered the house. Jimmy Craig had already left to catch a train home. Stewart had told him he couldn't be part of this, even though Joe was his son. There could be no personal involvement.

Reluctantly, Craig knew Stewart was right, and a patrol car had dropped him off at Haymarket.

They got the all clear, left the car and walked the short distance to the big house.

The old woman who owned the place was sitting in the living room, and rather than being shocked and weepy, like Harry thought he'd find her, she was quite excited.

'Nothing like this has happened round here that I can remember,' she said.

'Something to chat about at the Rotary,' Harry said.

She nodded. 'Oh yes. That Patricia one has nothing to brag about that's as good as this. Now sit down and tell me all about Melissa.'

Harry sat while Stewart made twirling motions

with his finger at the side of his head behind the woman's back.

'Let me ask you about Melissa,' Harry said, ignoring Stewart.

'She was starting a new job as a nurse over the road. Very nice girl. She said that she wanted somewhere to stay as she was selling her house in Fife.'

'Did she say whereabouts in Fife?' Harry asked.

'Oh yes.'

When she told him, he excused himself and called Craig.

'I think you need to get your team together, Jimmy. You might have a problem at your end.'

TWENTY-TWO

Eve was sitting in the passenger seat of her car at Dalgety Bay train station, her eyes red and watery. A bunch of paper hankies were in the footwell.

'Christ, Jim, what happened?' she said when Craig got in behind the wheel. He had to move the seat back before he could fully get in.

'A woman who had just started the job took Joe from the hospital.'

'Why? Why would she do that? Do you know who she is?'

'Her name is Melissa Thompson. We don't know who she is or why she took him. She used to work in Kirkcaldy and by all accounts was a nice girl.'

'Was she a previous girlfriend of Joe's?' Eve asked.

'I don't know. We'll go down to the house and I'll get my car. I'm assuming you're not going back to work?'

'I told Chris I'm taking the rest of the day off. They have a sub in there. He understands.'

'Right, let's go.'

He drove the five minutes to their house and they went inside. Karen was there with the dog. Finn was all over them before Craig calmed him down.

'I know my wife's home, but would you mind staying with the dog? We have a family emergency,' Craig said to her.

'No, that's fine. I'll just do what I normally do.'

'Thank you, I appreciate it.' He went through to the bedroom, where Eve was lying down.

'I would quite happily take knowing my little boy was in the psychiatric unit, because I would know he's safe,' she said.

'He wasn't that safe, given that somebody was able to take him out,' Craig replied.

'Do you think he went willingly?'

'I don't know to be honest. In his mental state, I think he could have easily been manipulated. For what reason, I don't know. I want to go and ask Carrie, see if she knows the woman who went into the hospital.'

'Okay, go and do that.'

'I'll be keeping in touch with Harry McNeil in Edinburgh.'

Eve nodded. 'Keep me in the loop, Jimmy.'

'I will. Love you.' He leaned over and kissed her.

Then he left and got into his own car and drove along the coastal road to Kirkcaldy, calling Dan on the way.

'Can you meet me at Carrie Dickson's house? I'm on my way there now.'

'DSup Baker told us what was going on over in Edinburgh. We'll do anything we can to make sure your son is safe.'

'Thanks, Dan. I won't be long.' Craig hung up and called DI Max Hold. 'Max? I need you to have somebody do some research.' He told him what he wanted.

Fifteen minutes later, he was booting it along to Carrie's house near the hospital. He remembered her saying she was going to Edinburgh and wondered if she had already left.

When he got there, Dan and Isla were parked outside the house. He pulled in behind them.

He got out and the cold enveloped him. Dan and Isla got out from the warmth of their car and approached him.

'I rang the bell, but there was no answer,' Dan said. 'We decided to wait on you.'

'Did you have a look in through the windows?'

'I did,' Isla said. 'There's net curtains up and it's hard to see inside, but it didn't look as if there was anybody home.'

'I remember Carrie saying that her neighbour next door would help out by coming round and checking on her grandfather before he died. I wonder if she still has the key. Let me go and knock, see if she's in. She's retired, so hopefully.'

He walked next door to the pensioner's house and knocked. A few minutes later, an old woman appeared, opening her door with the chain on.

'Yes?'

Craig held up his warrant card. 'DCI Craig. I was here when Albert died next door. I was wondering if you still had the key so we could go in and have a look. We're looking for the occupant and we want to make sure she's okay.'

'Oh yes, of course. Give me a sec, son. I still have a key here.' The door closed and opened again, minus the chain.

'I remember Carrie saying you were round when her grandfather died.'

Craig knew the old man had been murdered, but

as there was no proof and his killer was dead, he didn't bring it up. He took the key from her. 'I'll bring it right back.'

'Okay, son. I'm not going anywhere.'

Craig walked over to the door. 'Keep your eyes peeled. We don't know who this Melissa Thompson is, or why she took Joe, but she might have a grudge against Carrie.'

He unlocked the door and stepped inside.

'After you,' Dan said to Isla.

'Chivalry's not dead after all.'

'You're younger and faster.'

'Which means I can outrun you if there's somebody in there with an axe.'

'Yeah, watch me.'

They went into the house and Craig was glad he didn't smell death. The house smelled clean and fresh, which made sense since Carrie wanted to sell the house.

'Split up. Let's check the rooms,' Craig said.

He walked towards the stairs, which the old man had been pushed down just weeks earlier, and went up to the bedrooms. He could see Carrie's clothes were still in the wardrobe. Nothing looked out of place. Then he heard Dan shouting from downstairs.

He moved quickly, not taking two stairs at a time but giving the impression he was.

'Dan!' he shouted.

'In here!' Isla replied.

Craig rushed into the room expecting to find either a body or his son. It was neither.

'What's going on?' he asked, his heart racing.

There was a single bed in this room, and Craig remembered that Carrie's grandfather had stayed on the ground floor because he struggled to get up the stairs given that he walked with a Zimmer frame.

'Look round the other side of the bed, sir,' Isla said.

Craig slowly walked forward and saw what she was looking at.

Blood on the carpet. A small amount, as if there had been a nosebleed. As if somebody had punched Carrie on the nose.

'Call it in, Dan. Get forensics to test it.'

'Will do.'

'Where the hell is Carrie?' he said. *And is she still alive?* he thought.

Then Max Hold called him.

TWENTY-THREE

Adam Langston felt at home here. After all, he'd worked here for five years, before the Church had uprooted him. He had felt peace in this place, and the parishioners were nice to him.

The night before, he had walked up and down the street for a bit, trying to look inconspicuous, which he mainly was. If anybody had stopped and looked at him suspiciously, he would have said he had come back to pay his respects to his dead friend. When they saw the dog collar, they would immediately have dropped their guard.

It had been bitterly cold and he had even given thought to nipping into the pub along the road, but that wouldn't do at all. That would just be giving them a heads-up.

Besides, he knew for a fact that Vince kept his place looking like a distillery. And a brewery.

There had been no police tape across the driveway when he arrived, late at night. He had driven past a couple of times, just to make sure there was no polis hanging around. It was deserted, no sign of any activity at all, so he had parked his car outside the wee cottage next to the school. He knew the old woman who lived there, and if she had come out, he would have told her that he was just paying his respects to Vince.

There had been police tape over the front door, and he had pulled one side off, letting it hang down so it looked like it had just come loose. And since Vince had asked him to keep a spare key for the new lock on the front door, Adam didn't have to tan a window to get into the house.

Inside, the place had smelled awful. When he and Pamela had stayed over at Christmas, the place had smelled of old fish suppers and booze. Now it smelled like a rat had died.

He had walked into the living room, turning on a small lamp. The light might have been visible through the stained-glass windows of course, but it wasn't as if there were a lot of people going about. Maybe the old sod next door, but Adam couldn't care less now. His main objective in life was to stay alive.

He had been drawn to the pool table, where Vince had been murdered. He hadn't known the exact details, but it had been left behind for anybody to see. The blood had dried into the felt surface, and looking at it made him feel sick.

He had opened Vince's drinks cabinet and toasted his friend. He would miss him, and although he didn't want to see Pamela again, he admitted to himself that he would miss her too.

He had fallen asleep on the couch and woken up with a headache, a dry mouth and a longing to know if Pamela was still alive. But he told himself that there was nothing he could have done to save her. He had been in Dunfermline and Pamela was in Edinburgh.

He wondered if he would have been dead now if he hadn't escaped. He knew what they were after. It had to be that. There was never a whisper about what had happened, and as soon as Pamela had made that stupid Facebook post, that had got the ball rolling.

Part of him was afraid because somebody was with Pamela, hurting her even, but the other half was thinking, *Well, it was your own fucking fault.*

In his gut, he knew that the deaths of the spouses – and Vince's girlfriend – had been at the hands of those two guys who had wanted to hurt them both. It didn't make sense. Why would they kill their partners first, then come for Terry and Vince and Pamela? There was only one plausible explanation: it was a threat.

Adam didn't have anybody the men could kill as a threat, and if they were working their way through a list, he was obviously on that list.

Now he would have to make plans to disappear. Which was going to be hard, because all his belongings were in the church in Dunfermline. He could risk going back of course, like he had taken a risk sleeping with Pamela. Or he could do the easy thing and call somebody. It was that or run for the rest of his life.

And who wanted to run for the rest of their life?

TWENTY-FOUR

'Where are we going?' Joe asked again.

'I've got us the perfect place. For now.'

'I can't wait for this medicine to wear off. It's making me feel queasy.'

'It will, love,' Carrie said.

'Where did you get the name Melissa Thompson from?' he said, winding the window down.

'I made it up,' she lied. 'Now don't play with the windows, Joe, there's a good boy.'

He was acting like somebody who'd just had all their wisdom teeth pulled and was slowly coming out of anaesthesia. She knew she was going to have to keep giving him medicine until they were far away. Then she could work on getting Joe back again.

She drove the VW Golf along the esplanade looking over the sea to Edinburgh. The traffic in Kirkcaldy was light as she drove along, Joe slinking down in the seat like she told him.

'Are we going back to your house?' he asked her.

'No, I'm afraid not, Joe. We can't go back there.'

'Why not?'

'You know where you've just come from, right?'

He laughed. 'I suppose that wouldn't be a good idea.' He looked at her, still slumped down. 'So where are we going?'

'You'll find out in a minute.'

When Carrie had been in the hospital doing her orientation, they'd had her read through the patient files, so she could familiarise herself with them. She had taken a great interest in Joe's file. It seemed that Houdini was becoming more active by the day, but she would control that. She hoped.

She didn't have a Plan B if she couldn't.

Yet in the back of her mind, she knew there was only one way to deal with Houdini.

Her phone rang and she didn't want to get pulled over by the police for being on her phone while driving, so she found a place to park and answered it.

'Hello.'

The person on the other end talked to her for a few minutes.

'I'll be right there. Fifteen minutes, tops.'

Then she drove away again.

TWENTY-FIVE

Eve couldn't nap, no matter how hard she tried. She got up and made herself and Karen a cup of coffee, and then went back to her bed. Finn wanted to come with her, but she gently closed the door on him. She wanted to do some work in peace and he would only want to come on the bed with her and spread himself out.

She took her laptop out, sat it on her legs and opened it up to the Ancestry Tree website. She had joined after she had found out who Joe's biological mother was.

To find out that Joe had a personality disorder disturbed her on so many levels, but it explained a lot about his behaviour growing up. He would have tantrums a lot, and then suddenly he would stop and smile at her. She had thought that he had known it was wrong to throw a tantrum and was smiling apologetically.

Now she knew differently.

Inside him was another personality, one that was playing with his brain, waiting to get out. And unbeknownst to them, that other persona had come out under the guidance of his mother, herself a prolific killer.

Eve had said that she could create an account and would keep an eye out for any results.

There hadn't been any the last time she checked. Now she was curious, in case there was a whole clan out there. She logged in and navigated to the page she wanted.

And a name appeared.

Melissa Thompson.

DCI Mickey Thompson's daughter.

TWENTY-SIX

DSup Mark Baker pulled into the side of the road like his arse was on fire and jumped out of the car as fast as a man in his fifties with a dodgy knee could jump out.

'Mother of Christ,' he said, storming into the house. Craig was just finishing a phone call.

'Sir.'

'You've had a busy day, Jimmy,' Baker said. 'I'm not saying trouble follows you around, but I doubt anybody's going to be rubbing your heid for luck any time soon.'

'They still haven't found my son, but they're on it,' Craig replied, without adding *sarky bastard* at the end.

'Aye, sorry, son. I'm just frazzled and worried

about Carrie now you've called in the techs. Lazy bastards are probably having a fag break or something.'

'I'm sure they're busy. They won't pull out all the stops because of some blood on the carpet.'

'How big is the mess on the carpet?' Baker asked.

'It's not much, but something happened here. Like maybe she got belted in the face and her nose burst.'

'Let me see,' he said, and waited for Craig to lead the way. Craig obliged and took him to Albert's old room and pointed out the blood.

'We can be thankful there's not arterial spray up the wall,' Baker said.

'That would mean changing the wallpaper right enough,' Craig said.

'As it is, there's a chance she's alive. Whoever took her didn't kill her here. I mean, he might have wanted to incapacitate her, or else he could have strangled her or broken her neck or used any other means of killing her.' Baker looked at Craig. 'Do you think Joe came over here and got revenge or something?'

'I hope not. It's not something I want to think about. But listen, I asked Max to do some research work for me.'

'Aye. Lazy bastard farmed it out to Gary Menzies and Jessie Bell. He'd better be pulling his weight on the team, let me tell you.'

'Max called me with something they found out.'

'Oh? That Tim Hortons coffee is better than Starbucks? That laddie will be pissing coffee if he drinks any more.'

Craig wanted to tell the DSup to shut up and listen for a moment, but held back. 'Something else. There were names on the back of an old group photo that the victims were in. And a date. From fifteen years ago. It was taken in Pitlochry. Gary told me he did a search, and back then a young girl, aged sixteen, went missing and she's never been found. Those students from St Andrews were there in Pitlochry the night she went missing. They were questioned, but nothing came of it.

'One of her younger brothers spoke to the police and said he thought he saw a figure being bundled into the back of a car by a man, in the car park near the playing field. It was dark. He didn't know what kind of car, or what the man looked like, or indeed if it was a person or just a large holdall. He was dismissed and nothing ever came of it.'

'What's the girl's name? The one who went missing.'

JOHN CARSON

'Sandra Gibson. Her parents were called Adam and Eve.'

'Adam and Eve?'

'Yes,' Craig said. 'I bet they got ribbed about that.'

'Pardon the pun.' Baker shook his head. 'And nothing was heard from her again?'

'Vanished off the face of the earth. The students were questioned of course, but none of them saw anything. They were hanging around on the stadium seating.'

'And of course, those students who were there are our victims,' Baker said.

'Yes, they were there,' Craig replied. 'They all had an alibi, which was basically that they were all together.'

'Could have been some random nutter passing through. We both know that sort of thing happens.'

'We do,' Craig said. 'And it makes it so much harder to find the missing person.'

'If it was a random nutter, then he's been on the loose all this time.'

'However, with the dead crow being left on our first victim, and the rugby team being called The Crows, I tend to think that maybe this isn't the work of a random stranger.'

208

'Good point.'

'Gary gave me the address of the Gibsons at the time. He says the house is still in their name. It's an isolated wee place outside Pitlochry.'

'Let's go and give it a once-over then. It won't take long to get up there. I'll put my blues on and we can be up there in no time.'

Craig's insides churned at the thought of Baker driving them up there. 'Why don't I drive?'

'Pish.'

'Maybe we should take Dan along, just in case.'

'Just in case what? We need somebody to push the car when it breaks down?'

'We're looking for somebody who broke a pool cue in a man's eye socket.'

Baker looked past Craig. 'Dan! With us.' Then to Craig: 'Leave Isla your car keys in case she has to move the car.'

'Oh, the keys to the shiny new Volvo,' Isla said, coming to get Craig's keys. He handed them over.

'Baby her,' he said.

'Oh, and a wee *Lego Batman* keyring. Classy.' She smiled at him. 'Now, remind me, what's the middle pedal for?'

'Go away with yourself.'

They left the house and headed for Baker's car,

the DSup mumbling something like, *Thank fuck she's not driving my car*.

'Have you been in a car with Heid-the-Baw yet?'

'I heard that Stevenson,' Baker said, blipping the remote at his car.

'I haven't had the pleasure,' Craig said to Dan.

'Using the term loosely. Strap in and hold on.'

'He hears you slagging him off, but he never has you on the carpet.'

Dan laughed. 'I just wind him up. We go for a pint regularly. We were chasing somebody at Anstruther harbour one day and the dafty fell in. He can't swim. So I jumped in and pulled him out. Saved his life.' He nodded. 'Aye, that's me, lifesaver Dan. Saved your life twice, his once. I feel like I'm a lucky Irish leprechaun.'

'You look like a fucking leprechaun,' Baker said, more to himself than Dan.

They got in the car, and as soon as Baker took off, Craig felt like reaching for the sick bag.

TWENTY-SEVEN

Carrie pulled into the church car park and parked the Golf next to Adam's car.

'Where are we?' Joe asked.

'A friend of mine is going to help us, Joe. Come on, let's not keep him waiting.'

They got out, and Carrie helped Joe walk as he was still a bit unsteady on his feet. The car park still had snow on it, but it had been churned up by tyres and boots.

She opened the door to the church and they walked into the vestibule, where it was cool but not as cold as outside.

'This is a church,' Joe said, looking around the small area.

'It is. Let's go inside.' She opened the main door

and they walked into the heat. There was no sign of Adam.

'Hello?' she said, not too loudly but loud enough.

A side door opened and a man she hadn't seen in a very long time came out.

'Oh, Adam,' she said, rushing forward and hugging him. He held her close, squeezing her tightly, before finally letting her go.

Joe was standing there swaying slightly. She looked at Adam. 'This is Joe.'

Adam walked forward and stuck out a hand for him to shake. 'Hello, Joe. Carrie's told me all about you.'

'Has she now? Whoop-de-fucking-do.'

Carrie's eyes went wide and then she closed them for a second. 'Joe, let's get you something to drink. Are you thirsty?'

'Yes, I am.'

'Adam, do you have some water that Joe could drink?'

'Of course. Through in the kitchen.'

He led the way through to the back and poured Joe a glass of water, then handed it to Carrie, not wanting to stand too close to the psycho. Carrie handed it to Joe, who downed it in one go.

'More,' he said, holding the glass out. Carrie

stepped forward to take the glass and Joe pulled it back to his chest.

'No, not you. Him.' Joe locked eyes with Adam, who slowly stepped forward and put a hand out.

'Boo!' Joe shouted, and Adam jumped back. Joe laughed. 'Fucking look at you!' He laughed and walked over to the sink.

Carrie making eye contact with Adam. 'Joe's gone,' she said, her voice barely a whisper.

'What are you two whispering about?' Joe said after he'd filled his glass. He chugged it down and filled the glass again. 'I asked you a question, Adam.' He emphasised the name, spittle flying from his lips.

'Nothing,' Carrie said.

'Didn't sound like nothing to me.' He drank the water more slowly, locking eyes with Adam.

'It was nothing,' Adam said. 'Are you hungry?'

'Do I look like I'm fucking hungry?'

'No, you do not.' *I just said that to annoy you.*

'Well then. When I'm hungry, you'll be the first to know.' Joe finished the glass of water. 'I need a piss,' he said.

'That water goes through you quickly,' Adam said, smiling.

'From earlier, dumb fuck,' Joe said, taking a step

forward, but it wasn't really Joe. Joe was inside his own brain now, and Houdini was out for the day.

They all stood in silence looking at each other.

'Well?' Houdini said. 'Is somebody going to show me where the fucking toilet is?'

'Oh yes, it's upstairs. Turn right and it's at the end, facing you.'

They went back to the living room and Houdini walked along to the spiral staircase, passing the pool table.

'What happened here?' He stopped to look at the pool table.

'Something got spilled,' Adam said.

'Spilled? That's going to take some fucking cleaning there, pal.' Houdini carried on, climbing the spiral staircase, thumping his feet on the metal as he went.

'Here we go, up the wooden hill to bedtime land,' he sang, then he laughed out loud when he got to the top.

'Are you sure this is going to work?' Adam said, biting his lower lip.

'I hope so.' She hugged him again. 'Oh, Adam, why did you ever become a priest? We could have been so good together.'

'I know. I was running away.' He kissed her. 'Does he know about us? About our past?'

Carrie shook her head. 'No. And he won't. Now, did you do as I asked?'

Adam nodded. 'Yes, it's in the bathroom in plain sight. Hopefully, he'll see it and want to play with it.'

'I don't think he'll have a problem using a hammer,' Carrie said.

They could hear Houdini whistling now.

TWENTY-EIGHT

The journey by car would have taken a sane person around an hour, depending on traffic, weather and driving skills.

It took DSup Baker just under forty minutes, pedal to the floor. Craig wondered what it would feel like to simultaneously suffer a heart attack and shite himself. Dan sat in the back with his eyes closed and his earphones locked onto his phone, humming along to a tune only he could hear, and one Craig didn't recognise. Maybe it was one of the hymns they'd be playing at the crematorium after Baker killed them all.

At Craig's suggestion, they had contacted Perth HQ and had an armed response unit come up with them, and the big SUV had been waiting at the Mercedes dealership just outside the city and had followed them up.

The House of Bruar mail order warehouse came at them in a flash, and for a moment Craig thought that Baker had fallen asleep at the wheel, but then he cleared his throat and all was well. He took the slip road, turned left at the roundabout and crossed the River Tummel.

'It's a tiny road up here on the right, so keep your eyes peeled,' Baker said. He looked in his rear-view mirror, craning his neck to see Dan. 'Look out!' he shouted, and grinned when Dan jumped.

'What the hell?' he said.

'Keeping you on your toes.'

'Daft bastard,' Dan said. 'I nearly shat myself. And Taylor Swift was up next on my playlist.'

'Now, look out for a wee road on the right.'

'Like that one?' Craig said, pointing.

'Oh shite,' Baker said, slamming on the brakes and hauling the wheel. Dan looked out the back window to see if the ARU driver was cursing them out, but he wasn't. A logging truck up their arse would have been fun.

Baker booted it up the single-track road, oblivious to any other traffic coming towards them, but they were lucky – there was none.

'It's up on the right-hand side. Literally in the middle of nowhere,' Baker said. 'There it is.' He drove under a short canopy of trees that hung over the road and pulled over, the ARU right behind.

They all got out.

'I'm not sure if the bloke who lives here is in danger or not, but he reported an abduction when he was twelve. Somebody's been going around killing people from that time. He might be a target, or he might not, but let's check anyway. There's been no answer on the landline, and we don't have any other number. His name is Dale Gibson.'

'You want us to go in first in case there's a threat?' the first armed officer said.

'You can stand behind us ready to take over. But be aware of your surroundings. The guy who's been killing in Fife is a nutter.'

They stood in the gloom, the trees shading them from the sunlight, looking at the property. There was a gate at the end of the driveway and no sign of any cars. The small garage beyond the gate was open and empty. The house was over on the right, a stone-built affair that looked like it could have been a hunting lodge back when Queen Victoria came to this neck of the woods. Smoke drifted lazily from the single chimney on the house.

'Christ, this is like a horror movie,' Dan said.

Craig undid the latch on the gate and walked over to the front door, Baker and Dan behind, followed by the two armed officers. The driver was still in the car, as per protocol.

As Craig approached the front door, they heard a shout from inside. A man's voice, raised. Then a scream.

He tried the door handle and it turned, the door opening easily. Another scream, coming from the room on the left.

Craig burst in, followed by the armed officers.

'Put the fucking knife down!' an armed officer shouted.

The man was several feet away from the woman, who was tied to a chair. He looked at her.

'Don't do it, son. You'll never make it,' Craig said.

Dale Gibson, the man who had been given the moniker Abel by his classmates after they found out his mum and dad were called Adam and Eve, decided he was going to try it anyway.

One shot tore through his heart before he had a chance to bring the knife down.

Pamela Armstrong sobbed with relief as Craig went over to her. He untied her from the chair.

'Hello, Pamela. You remember me, DCI Craig from Fife?'

'I do,' she replied, sniffing back the tears.

'I think it's time you told me what's going on.'

Then his phone rang.

TWENTY-NINE

Carrie and Adam were sitting on the couch when he came. David Gibson, the man who had been nick-named Cain all his life.

'Well, well, the last two,' he said. 'You're a hard man to track down, Adam. I thought you and Carrie were hiding out in old Mickey Thompson's house. He is your biological father, isn't he? Your mother certainly put it around. Is that why Mickey paid for you to go to St Andrews Uni? Must have been. I didn't know the bloke, obviously, but hats off to him. And now here we are, so no worries. You mind if I join your little soirée?'

Adam stood up. 'You need to leave. You've done enough damage.'

Cain laughed. 'You'd like that, wouldn't you? For

me to just skip out of here and leave you two love-birds alone. That's not going to happen, Adam. As much as you and Carrie here would like that.'

'It's Melissa actually,' Carrie said. 'I'm using a different name now.'

'I can imagine,' Cain said.

'How did you know where we were?' Adam said.

'Our little friend Pamela sang like a songbird. Not like a crow, mind, but she told me you used to be a priest here. I didn't know that when we killed Vince.'

'You killed the others, didn't you?' Adam said.

Something changed in Cain then, a slight shift in his persona. 'I only wanted to find out who killed our sister and where you buried her.'

'I killed her,' Carrie said. 'It was an accident.'

'They all say that.'

'It was. The festivities were going on late and the others in the team had gone to a pub, leaving our small group alone. Sandra came along and wanted a drink. We told her she was underage, but she said she had already been drinking. She wanted more. She got aggressive and slapped me and tried to grab my beer, but I pushed her away. She fell off the stadium seating and we all heard a crack. When we went down to see to her, her eyes were open, but she didn't have a pulse. We were all scared it would ruin the rest of our lives, so Adam took her away in his car.'

Cain laughed. 'You expect me to believe that? My brother said he saw you alone putting her in the car.' He pointed to Adam.

'That's because I told the others to leave. It was an accident, David.'

'Her life ended, but you all got to go on with yours! That's fucking fair, is it?'

'It happened because she was there. She was sixteen. She shouldn't have been drinking and she shouldn't have been wandering about. Where were your parents?'

'Don't you fucking dare blame them! They were good people. It wasn't often they got to go out. They trusted Sandra to behave, though she was always arguing with them. But she didn't deserve to die.'

'Nobody deserved to die! Not our friends!' Adam shouted. 'Did you kill their spouses? Kill Vince's girlfriend?'

David locked eyes with him. 'Yes. We killed them. We wanted your friends to suffer before we asked them where our sister is. And you know what? If Vince had told us, he wouldn't have died on that pool table.'

'He didn't know! None of them did! Only I know, and I can tell you where she is if you'll let Carrie go.'

Cain looked at one then the other. 'Tell me first and I'll let you both walk away.'

Adam nodded. 'I buried her in the woods just outside the car park at that trail opposite where you live. Near the signpost. Take a few steps in and you'll find her there.'

'I don't believe you,' Cain said. 'So here's what I'm going to do: I'm going to kill her first, then you'll tell me where my sister is and then you can walk away.'

'This ice cream is pretty good,' Craig said, walking out of the kitchen holding a bowl and eating ice cream with a spoon.

Cain turned to him. 'Who the fuck are you?'

Craig ate some more ice cream. 'You really should try some.'

'I asked you a question,' Cain said, stepping closer.

He didn't see Joe coming down the spiral staircase.

'Oh yes, I forgot. I'm DCI Craig, and you're under arrest.'

'That's right, son. You're going nowhere,' another figure said, stepping out of the office.

Cain turned to look at him.

'I'm Detective Superintendent Mark Baker. Ditto what he said. About you being under arrest, not the ice cream bit.'

Cain flew at Craig. He had been expecting such a reaction, and he threw the bowl hard at Cain's face when he was a few steps away. The ceramic bowl bounced off his nose, and Cain let out a yell, but he carried on.

Joe ran over. Adam tried to stop him, but he easily skirted him, and as Craig and Cain were going at it, he grabbed Cain and spun him round, lifting the hammer.

'Joe! No!' Craig said, and something flickered in Joe's eyes. An internal conflict between Joe and Houdini.

Baker walked up behind Cain and kicked him hard between the legs. Cain yelled and went down like a felled tree. 'Jesus, this floor is a bit uneven. Did you see that? I lost my balance.'

Craig grabbed the hammer from Joe as Baker took his handcuffs out. When Cain was safely in cuffs, he got on the radio. 'Get them in here.'

Joe sat down on the floor and crossed his legs and started rocking back and forth.

Uniforms rushed in led by Dan Stevenson, who grabbed Carrie and put her in cuffs. Adam was led out of the house, to be questioned along the road in Glenrothes.

'You're Joe's sister,' Craig said to Carrie. 'You told us you were boyfriend and girlfriend.'

'We made that up. I am his sister. I wanted to take him away and start a new life,' she said.

'How were you going to do that? He's mentally ill.'

'We would have managed.'

Craig shook his head. 'Are there any more of you out there?'

'That's for me to know and you to find out,' she said.

Then Dr Solomon came in and knelt down beside Joe. 'Come on, let's get you back to your nice warm room. I have some of your friends here.' A couple of attendants walked in and they helped Joe to his feet.

'I wasn't going to let him hurt you, Dad,' he said.

Craig didn't know if he meant Cain or Houdini.

THIRTY

It was windy but dry as Craig stood in the cemetery with Isla. The gravediggers had done their thing, the big JCB moving the dirt with ease.

It had taken some time to get the exhumation order, but ultimately Lou Renwick had given permission. So they had organised everything and promised him that his wife's coffin would be treated with the greatest respect.

Now, the JCB lifted the coffin out of the grave and gently laid it down on the ground. Then some of Stan Mackay's team jumped in and started digging.

'Do you think she'll be there?' Isla asked.

'Adam Langston was quite convincing when he said he buried Sandra Gibson in that grave before Mrs Renwick's funeral. He had known from Susan that her mother had died and the funeral was going to be soon after Sandra died in Pitlochry. He figured nobody would ever know and Sandra would be listed as a missing person forevermore.'

Isla nodded. 'If only Pamela Armstrong hadn't organised the reunion, none of them would have died.'

One of the techs raised a hand and a white-suited Mackay went across to the grave, spoke to him and turned to Craig.

'She's there,' he said simply.

THIRTY-ONE

A week later

'Is there anything else that's going to affect our family, Jim?' Eve Craig asked her husband. They were sitting at the little table in their living room, looking out over the dark sea to the lit bridges, Finn at their feet.

'There's nothing left, sweetheart. I think we've been put through the mill, but at least Joe is safe again, and they're monitoring his meds and he's doing well.'

'There's such a lot going on, isn't there? The firearms team shooting that scumbag in Pitlochry. All the other stuff.' She looked at him. 'Sometimes I start to feel overwhelmed by it all. Especially when I think of that woman and her offspring. I never thought for one moment that Carrie was his sister.'

'You wouldn't, though, would you? He said she was his girlfriend. We thought she was a good bit older than him, but to be honest I was getting used to the idea. Sometimes it's not age that matters. But she had been playing with his brain and inside, his alter ego was coming out and there was conflict in his mind. That's what the doctor said.'

'I hope that bloody hospital has got its act together.'

'There are new procedures in place. Besides, Carrie used her original name at work; that's why she was able to supply references. It was all very well planned.'

'I hope they throw away the key.'

Craig felt the whisky kick in. It was taking the edge off. 'On another note, Karen said she's finished the first draft of her new book and she asked if either of us would fancy reading it. I said we both would. I really hope she makes it big with this one.'

'She's written before?'

'Yes. She said she wrote books that will live in a

drawer for the rest of her life, never to see the light of day again. It's how writers cut their teeth.'

'Good for her. I'll read it.' She looked at him. 'Maybe I'll write a book about what happened to us.'

He smiled. 'I don't think anybody would ever believe it.'

AFTER WORD

First of all, I would like to thank Jacqueline Beard who has a better set of eyes than me! Thanks also to Lisa McDonald and to Gary Menzies for letting me use his name. And to my wife and family, my greatest supporters.

And especially to you, the reader, for coming along.

If you could see your way to leaving a review or a rating, that would be really helpful. Thank you in advance.

If you want to write to me, please do. Go to my website and use the contact button there and I'll get back to you as soon as.

www.johncarsonauthor.com

Stay safe my friends.

John Carson

Printed in Great Britain
by Amazon

48531081R00148